# Sanctuary Isle

# SANCTUARY ISLE

## Bill Knox

Constable • London

First published in Great Britain 1962
This edition published in Great Britain 2002
by Constable, an imprint òf Constable & Robinson Ltd
3 The Lanchesters, 162 Fulham Palace Road
London W6 9ER
www.constablerobinson.com

ISBN 1–84119–590–1

Printed and bound in Great Britain

A CIP catalogue record for this book
is available from the British Library

# Chapter One

The seabird had travelled far, and was weak. Full five thousand miles lay behind it, north and west from the burning heat of a beach on the coast of Angola, across the Gulf of Guinea, round Dakar and the haunch of Africa. Near Madeira, the sudden shattering violence of an electrical storm had separated it from the hundreds of other roseate terns on the long, straining flight north. But the lone tern had kept on, grey wings beating a chosen path, fighting through a gale off Biscay, sometimes blown miles off that invisible line, always returning, always heading northwards.

But now the journey was almost over. As the sun sank low, the bird sensed the growing nearness of its goal. A sensitive combination of instinct and memory turned its flight a point to the west. The sun, beginning to set now, danced its rays over the water far below, glanced skywards, and suddenly the tern's white breast feathers showed the underlying warm red sheen of its kind.

The tern was weary. Three summers had passed since it hatched to life among the rock and salt-stunted grass of the island ahead. But now the wing-beat increased a fraction then slowed as, triumphant, the bird went into a long shallow dive, yielding itself completely to the magnetic compulsion of the sea-fringed outcrop.

Dusk was falling. The tall white bulk of a lighthouse tower sent out its first stabbing fingers of white. The tern circled, low now, ignoring the villainous clamour of a black-headed gull, the sudden skyward sparking of a long-

5

legged oyster-catcher. There were other terns below, hundreds of them, scattered and resting in small colonies over the length and breadth of the little island.

The newcomer veered beyond the lighthouse, used one wing-beat and an air-current to carry it past a frowning line of granite rocks, and settled to rest on a stretch of pebbles just beyond.

Fatigue made the tern dull to possible danger. The bird took a few weary steps forward, seeking some handy, sheltering hollow, then gave a sudden squawk of fright and flapped skywards as a dark shape in the shadow of the rocks gave a sighing moan.

The tern was weary, too weary. Once again it settled on the pebbles and this time found the shielding hollow it craved. The little black head drooped low into its breast feathers, red legs pulled up tight and small beneath.

It had obeyed the urge, had made the journey. Now it must rest . . . and the dark shape so near was still. The tern's head fell forward.

Arm's length apart, man and seabird died with the coming of night.

The lighthouse beam probed its monotonous routine, a glaring eye sweeping seawards. A score of thousand birds settled into their nesting areas. Only the waves disturbed the silence.


With a plunge and buck, the small boat breasted through the trough and crest of yet another slow-rolling glass-green wave. Above, the mid-June sun shone warm and bright in a sky of brilliant blue, speckled here and there by a scudding cloudlet of cottonwool white. Ashore, there was all the glory of a perfect summer day – but out on the waters of the Firth of Lorne a strong, gusting wind made conditions less comfortable. From somewhere behind him, Chief Detective Inspector Colin Thane heard a gasp of abject misery.

'Thon wee inspector of yours is not over happy,' grinned

the fair-haired, stockily built young boatman, wiping a trickle of spray from his forehead with one sleeve of his faded blue overalls. Of the six passengers aboard his small command, four appeared to be reasonably happy. But the other two . . . he grinned again. Och well, why worry about policemen?

Colin Thane took another faceful of wind-blown sea-spray, forced a faint answering smile, then moved aft. The twenty-foot open launch, time-scarred, paraffin engine clanking beneath the battered wood of its midship housing, took another lurch and sent him staggering against the nearest huddled figure.

'Sorry, Phil –'

A white face turned towards him. Detective Inspector Phil Moss was saying nothing – he was afraid of the possible consequences of opening his tight-clamped lips. But the message in his eyes was sufficient. Phil Moss didn't care any more whether the little launch stayed afloat or not. His one remaining hope was that, sooner or later, he would quit this stretch of West Highland coast and return to the civilized knifings, safe-blowings and robberies of Millside Division, Glasgow.

Two more steps took Thane to the stern-sheets of the launch. He squeezed down between the two men already there.

'How much further?'

The smaller of the passengers, small and neat in well-worn tweeds, blinked sympathetically. 'We're more than two-thirds of the way across, Chief Inspector. Another ten minutes and we'll have reached Sanctuary Isle. There it is, straight ahead, where you can see the lighthouse tower.' He pointed one thin hand seawards. 'Now, look over there on your left – where the waves are breaking white. We call that The Fangs. It's a line of half-tide rock, covered over at the moment.'

'And well named, too,' growled the uniformed policeman by his side. Inspector Davidson of Argyll County Police frowned in the direction indicated. 'Half-tide or lower, and you'd see the reason. A long jaw of granite, ready to chew the heart out of any ship's hull. The automatic light on the Isle has put an end to most of the danger, it's true, but this is still a tricky stretch of water when the sea runs rough.'

'As it is now?' queried Thane.

Another curtain of spray drenched aboard, spattering Thane's lightweight city suit. But the Argyll man shook his head. 'Blame the boatman, not the weather,' he declared. 'Willie MacPherson is having a spot of fun at your expense. He knows I know it, too. If he wanted to steer a slightly longer course, take a tack or two and keep this tub bow-on to the waves, well, we wouldn't be taking half this thumping.' He glared for'ard, to where the boatman sat at seemingly innocent peace with the world, one hand patting the engine cover in time to the boat's erratic beat. 'We picked him up for a spot of trouble last summer – he was lucky to get off with a fine.'

'And now Willie's getting a bit of his own back.' Thane gave a dry chuckle as he examined the result. Phil Moss was still slumped in silent misery. Near the bow, Detective Superintendent Dan Laurence, the Glasgow C.I.D. scientific expert who had come north with them, appeared to be almost enjoying the sea-trip. His mop of white hair blown into rumpled confusion by the gusting wind, his bulky untidy form wedged tight in the bow thwart, he gave a cheerful wave in their direction. Beside him, however, the detective constable who acted as general fetcher and carrier was sprawled in an attitude of despair, head hanging over the side.

The sole civilian aboard, the little man in the well-worn tweeds, cleared his throat. 'Umh – after all, Inspector, you did say you wanted to get out as quickly as possible. Perhaps Willie is – er – just being enthusiastic.'

Thane saw the County man's face darken and decided it was time to change the subject. 'Whatever his reason, we'll soon be there,' he agreed. 'I'd like to know a little more about what happened. All I really have to work on is that

8

there's a dead man on this island, that it was murder, and that Argyll County passed on a request for help to Glasgow.'

The actual briefing, though a trifle more explicit, had still been meagre. In Glasgow that morning, Colin Thane had decided to devote his time to a long overdue blitz on the paperwork rapidly swamping his desk as Millside divisional C.I.D. chief. But ten minutes after he'd begun the task he'd received a telephone call from Headquarters. Buddha Ilford, the city's overall C.I.D. boss, never wasted words. A body had been found on Sanctuary Isle, four miles off the Argyll mainland in the Firth of Lorne, a point not very far south of the island of Mull. Sanctuary Isle was, appropriately enough, a bird sanctuary. The dead man had been warden and the island's only inhabitant. He'd died from poison and the county police were treating it as murder. Thane and Phil Moss were to go north with a Scientific Bureau detail, tidy up the matter with decent haste, and then return to normal duty as quickly as possible.

The car journey north from Glasgow to the little fishing village of Inverlay had taken a fraction over two and a half hours. Then they'd been bundled into the waiting boat. The paperwork would still be waiting when they got back.

Thane sighed. 'Mr Hollis, just how does your association fit into the picture?'

The smaller man, thin, in his late fifties and obviously nervous, blinked again. A chartered accountant, Edgar Hollis was devoted to the gentler aspects of life which did not normally include meeting policemen engaged in murder investigations. 'We have a lease of the Isle – it is part of the Corronel family estate. They own most of the lands around here.'

'We?' Thane's half-raised eyebrow completed the question.

'The Scottish Sea Bird Society,' explained the accountant. He clung to the edge of the launch's transom as it lurched sideways in yet another wave-trough, then added, 'I'm convenor of our Sanctuary Isle committee. This is our first season in occupancy at the Isle – and now this happens.' He shook his head. 'My Society will be shocked at the news. This was to have been the cumulation of so much work. And the seabirds –'

'Never heard of a bird being charged with murder,' grunted the Argyll policeman. 'What difference does it make to them?'

Hollis spread his hands wide, then grabbed the transom as another wave loomed up. 'Sanctuary Isle is, well, unique. The migrant bird population each summer is probably more varied than anywhere else in Britain.' His voice gained enthusiasm. 'Do you know, Chief Inspector, one of our members was out at the Isle last summer and identified a Bonelli's warbler and a pectoral sandpiper. Both exceedingly rare – in fact, it's only the second time a Bonelli has been sighted in this part of the world.'

'Nice for you,' agreed Thane dryly. 'So you decided to run the Isle as a sanctuary, and put a warden on it.'

Inspector Davidson flipped open his notebook. 'Name Lewis Tinemann, retired sea captain, age sixty-five. Home somewhere near Southport in England – Southport police are trying to locate relatives.'

'An excellent man,' agreed the Bird Society convenor. 'We advertised the appointment, and had over a hundred applicants – but Captain Tinemann was our obvious choice from the moment he got in touch with us.'

The County officer gave a grunt. 'Tinemann moved out here three weeks ago – just before the end of May. His job as warden was to keep a record of the types of birds nesting, patrol the Isle, and make sure no one landed without the Society's express permission. He lived in a small hut they've put up, and he was on his own. The Isle's normally uninhabited, and the only building – apart from the hut, that is – is the lighthouse. It's fully automatic, though a depot ship comes round every month or so to check over and refuel the gas tanks that feed the lamp.'

'Visitors?' queried Thane.

'Since he came out, just Mr Hollis here and few other Society members. Mr Hollis lives in Oban, and that's less than an hour's drive away. I asked him to meet us at Inverlay and come out, in case there might be some point he could help you clear up.'

It was, admitted Thane, a sensible idea. 'How about Tinemann? Did he have any kind of boat on the Isle?'

Davidson shook his head. 'No. Willie MacPherson was contracted to take a trip out once a week, ferrying supplies. His last regular trip was yesterday morning. But Tinemann asked him to come across again today. Seems he'd found some of his supplies were spoiled – contaminated by lamp-oil, he told MacPherson.

'Anyway, MacPherson took his boat across first thing this morning, just as he'd promised. When he reached the Isle there was no sign of Tinemann at the landing place – which was unusual. MacPherson waited by the launch for a spell, then decided to take a look around. The Isle is fairly small, and it didn't take long.'

'So he found the body!' Thane looked at their boatman with renewed interest.

'Aye.' Inspector Davidson raised his uniform cap sufficiently to allow him to scratch the crown of his close-cropped hair beneath, then sighed. 'Well, MacPherson could tell the man was dead, so he just left him where he was, came back across the water to Inverlay, and told the local police. They contacted me, and I went over with Doctor Connan from the village. Ach, I thought Tinemann had probably fallen and broken his neck. But young Connan sniffed around for a bit – he's new in these parts, and keen as mustard – then turned round and told me we'd a murder.'

Another lurch into a wave-trough was followed by a heavy shower of spray which swept the length of the launch. For once, Thane ignored the drenching discomfort.

'Cause of death?'

11

'Aconite poisoning,' said the Argyll man. 'Time of death, probably eleven p.m. yesterday. That's about all I know, to be honest – except that Doctor Connan says aconite is just about the most dangerous poison known.'

Thane nodded. 'Not the sort of stuff you keep around the kitchen. Where's the doctor? On the Isle?'

'No. He came back with me. Said he'd got all the immediate information there was, and some woman in Inverlay was expecting her first child to arrive at any moment. Ach, I'd have liked him to stay. But he said he thought it more important to bring a bairn into the world than to stand watch over a corpse.'

The engine note died away, the launch slowed, then swung on to a new course. Almost simultaneously, Thane noticed that the waves seemed to have lost much of their rolling menace. From his post at the engine housing the boatman gave a mischievous twinkle.

'Nearly there, gentlemen. A fast journey, eh, Inspector Davidson?'

The county officer nodded acid agreement.

Bright, almost dazzling clear in the brilliant sunshine, Sanctuary Isle lay less than three hundred yards distant, a narrow half-mile rock and sand shield which gave calm waters within its crescent-shaped bay. The Isle was a mere twenty feet above sea level at its highest point, a bare, low-lying mass of grey rock with a fringe of tall grass and long-stemmed weeds, all sturdy varieties which could withstand the biting salt spray and still find sufficient nourishment in the sparse pockets of sandy, pebble-specked soil.

Well within shelter now, the last pretence of the sea's anger left behind, the launch nosed in. Blue-green water chuckled under the bow as Willie MacPherson spun the tiny steering wheel and turned her towards a jutting plat-form of flat, natural granite. Two figures in police uniform scrambled over the boulders, reached the rock slab, and watched their approach.

In the bow, Dan Laurence's assistant began to show first

signs of a rewakened interest in life. Midships, Phil Moss raised a white face, looked around him, and sighed.

'How'd you feel, Phil?' queried Thane.

His second-in-command took out a cigarette, lit it with trembling fingers, and glared at their boatman. 'How about arresting him for assault on the police?'

'Och, it won't be so bad on the return trip,' soothed MacPherson. 'That's a promise.'

'Return trip?' Phil Moss raised anguished eyes sky-wards.

A series of splashes, loud in the relative silence, turned Thane's attention from his companion's misery. A family of seals had decided to move. Headed by a sharp-faced bristle-whiskered bull, they slid one by one from the rocks, took to the water, and headed in convoy out into the bay, only the tips of their heads in view.

The boatman thumbed towards them. 'More business for Preston,' he said. 'They'd do better to stay nearer shore.'

'Preston?' It was a new name to Thane.

'A shark-hunter. When sharks are scarce, he goes after seal,' said MacPherson. 'I saw his boat cruising around north o' the Isle as we came over.'

He turned his attention to manoeuvring the launch alongside the naturally-formed landing place. There was a deepwater channel leading right up to the edge of the huge granite slab, but only a few yards beyond the water was sufficiently clear to show the weed-encrusted rocks which lay not far below the surface.

MacPherson gauged his moment, then clashed the engine into reverse gear, moving the throttle forward at the same time. The ancient power-plant gave a rattling bellow, the propeller churned a halt to their forward drift, and then the boatman cut the ignition, scrambled to the bow, and tossed a line to one of the two policemen waiting on the rock. The rope was secured round a handy projection, the same drill was carried out with a second line from the launch's stern, and their journey had ended.

Thane stepped ashore with Phil Moss and Davidson,

then turned back to give Hollis a helping hand. The Bird Society official winced as he crossed from launch to shore. 'Thanks, Chief Inspector.' He sighed. 'I'm feeling pretty stiff-limbed today, I'm afraid. And I didn't get much sleep last night either, for an old familiar reason – a bout of neuralgia in my back.'

The two uniformed men had moved forward to meet the new arrivals. One, wearing sergeant's stripes, gave a sizzling salute to Davidson. 'All quiet, sir. Nothing to report, except that yon fellow Preston's boat has been cruising around.'

Inspector Davidson gave a nod. 'We saw it on the way across. Sergeant, this is Chief Inspector Thane, Glasgow C.I.D. He's taking over.'

The sergeant stiffened. 'Sergeant Stewart, sir. Inspector Davidson left me on guard duty with two men. One of them is standing by over beside the body.'

Thane introduced the rest of his party, then turned to the Bird Society convenor, who was standing a few paces distant.

'What's happened to all your seabirds, Mr Hollis?' he queried. 'Scared away by the uniforms?'

Half a dozen gulls were planing around the lighthouse tower. Otherwise, the sky was empty of life. But Hollis gave a weak smile, fumbled in one pocket of his tweed jacket, and startled the detective by producing an automatic pistol, showing as little concern as another man might have displayed in bringing out a handkerchief. Without a word, he fired two shots into the air. The sharp cracks brought an immediate, fantastic reaction.

With a mighty crying and a near thunderous flap of massed wings, several hundred seabirds exploded from the shelter of the rocks around. Their alarm cries were repeated and taken up afresh as hundreds then thousands more rose skywards, a spreading ripple of alarmed grey, white and black, the noise changing swiftly from fear to anger.

Mr Hollis put the pistol in his pocket and gazed sky-

14

wards, entranced. 'Beautiful . . . beautiful. A good season, Chief Inspector. Many are gulls, of course – see, there's a greater black-back – but there are any number of more interesting types, oyster-catchers, terns, pipits. Yes, an excellent season.'

Slowly, the birds began to settle again to their rocks and nests.

'There doesn't seem to be any shortage,' agreed Thane. 'But what about the pistol, Mr Hollis?'

The Bird Society man beamed. 'There are up to twenty thousand seabirds on the Isle, Chief Inspector. That's what makes it so important to the ornithologist.' Then he blinked. 'The pistol? Oh, it's licensed, of course, but only loaded with blanks. I always bring it when I come out here – it's useful when we want to scare some of the bigger gulls away from the nesting areas used by smaller birds.' He sniffed. 'Gulls! Some of them are no better than pirates.'

Sergeant Stewart edged into the conversation. 'I've been out here with Mr Hollis before, sir. We know about the pistol. Eh – would you like to see the body? And, well, if you don't mind a wee suggestion, sir –'

'Go ahead,' invited Thane.

'Well, sir, if the Scientific people wouldn't mind' – he carefully avoided Dan Laurence's gaze – 'maybe they'd like to start by having a look over the warden's hut. It's just a wee bit place beside the automatic light. Then, when they were finished, we could maybe use the stove to organize a cup of tea or something . . .' his voice trailed away and he waited, hopefully.

Thane grinned. 'Best idea I've heard yet. How about it, Dan?'

Superintendent Laurence placed the last piece of equipment over the shoulders of his already laden assistant.

'Good sense,' he rumbled. 'Come on, Johnny. There's work to be done.'

They set off over the rocks towards the light, Laurence in the lead, the long-suffering detective constable staggering

15

along behind, his burden of cases and containers bumping and thudding one against another.

Leaving the uniformed constable waiting by the launch, Thane's party headed in the opposite direction, scrambling over the rocks and through knee-high grass and thistle towards the southern tip of the Isle. Sergeant Stewart's right boot crunched on something small and brittle. He stopped, then shrugged. 'Sorry, Mr Hollis – that's one nest less. I just didna' see it.'

The Sea Bird Society official shook his head. 'It couldn't be helped, sergeant. But if you would, all move carefully please – this is one of the favourite nesting spots.'

They resumed their trek in Indian file. Thane heard a familiar low-pitched grumble from immediately behind him, and glanced over his shoulder.

'Feeling better, Phil?'

Detective Inspector Moss had recovered his natural complexion, which still seemed unhealthily pale against the outdoor tan of the Argyll officers in the party.

'I'll live,' he grudgingly agreed. 'It's the trip back that's worrying me. My ulcer's bad enough without any additional strain on my stomach lining.'

His further views on the condition of his ulcer, one of Millside Division's most famed and cherished possessions, had to wait.

'Watch this next bit,' warned Sergeant Stewart. 'There's a wee bit o' a drop down, and then you're at the place.'

The grass and weed gave way to bare, broken granite. A few yards on, and the rock ended as if cut short by some giant axe. There was a sudden drop of about eight feet, down to a beach-like surface which was a mixture of shingle and small boulders.

One by one, the men half-scrambled half-jumped to the lower level. At the bottom, the waiting uniformed constable hastily finished stubbing his cigarette and stood self-consciously beside the blanket-covered shape which lay close to the foot of the rock.

16

Thane went over, lifted the blanket, and inspected what lay beneath.

Captain Tinemann had died with his face to the sky. But his body, dressed in rubber seaboots, coarse serge trousers and a thick white double-knit wool jersey, was twisted to one side. His left hand rested on a large boulder as if he was still preparing to make one last attempt to rise to his feet.

Despite his years, Tinemann had been a sturdy, well-built figure, a fraction over the six-foot mark. Thane looked at the dead man again, then knelt on the shingle for a closer inspection of the bearded, heavily-jowled face, walnut brown from exposure to wind and sun, yet now with a strange blue tinge of colour beneath the tan.

Slowly, disliking the task, Thane checked the dead man's trouser pockets. The right-hand contained a heavy bone-handled clasp-knife with well-worn marlinspike, an old but relatively clean handkerchief, and a length of light-weight cord. The left yielded a storm-proof cigarette lighter, a packet of cigarettes and a police-type whistle. The hip pocket was empty.

'Not much there.' Moss crouched down beside him. 'There's a watch on his wrist – still going. No money?'

'Nowhere to spend it,' Thane reminded him, then glanced up at the granite rock above. 'He could have fallen from up there. The poor devil was probably staggering around wondering what had happened, and went over the edge.'

'Uh-huh.' Moss rose to his feet again. 'Not a happy way to die, wandering around an uninhabited island with a dose of poison inside you.'

'Sad – such a sad thing.' The words, said in a tone of carefully restrained emotion, came from Edgar Hollis. But the Bird Society official wasn't using them to mourn the death of his warden. In one hand, he held a small, limp bundle of grey and white feathers. 'A roseate tern, Chief Inspector Thane. I found it lying here, almost beside

17

Captain Tinemann's body. So sad – to fly all the way from Africa, just to die from exhaustion.'

'Equally sad for Captain Tinemann,' grunted Moss. 'Even if he only came up from Southport.'


There was little to be learned from the stretch of pebbled beach where Captain Tinemann had collapsed to die. Thane headed back towards the white pencil-shape of the lighthouse tower, Phil Moss by his side, the remainder of the party straggling behind them.

As a team, the two Millside Division detectives were in odd contrast, both in physique and outlook. But it was no haphazard chance that they regularly found themselves being allocated by Headquarters to carry out assignments which took them considerably beyond the boundaries of their divisional territory.

Tall, easy-moving and occasionally impetuous in his determination to follow a long-shot hunch, Thane was in his early forties – which made him a youngster among the majority of Chief Detective Inspectors. Dark-haired, his face cheerfully rugged, his muscular build admittedly a few pounds heavier than it had been ten years previously, Colin Thane was prepared to admit that his main weaknesses were a frequent lack of patience and a disrespect for both procedure and paperwork – at the same time as he had to admit that they added up to the disciplined, grinding mills of police routine which so often held the key to successful investigation.

Married with two children, a bungalow home with accompanying mortgage in a south side suburb of Glasgow and, a new possession, a large, young and perpetually hungry Boxer dog, he was, basically, a strongly human individual. But the humanity could give way, as now, to hard, controlled anger – and that was the time when Thane reached peak efficiency.

Detective Inspector Phil Moss, on the other hand, was thinner, older and with a grey outlook on the world in general. He barely met the minimum height requirements of the police medical, and was alleged to have squeezed through by quietly standing on tip-toe. A confirmed bachelor, his wry sense of humour served as only partial release for the inward tension of investigation – a tension which was the root cause of his grumbling stomach ulcer.

Grumbling ulcer, grumbling nature was too hasty a summary of Moss's character. When trouble loomed, his mood changed. Perhaps he lacked the long-distance logic of Thane. But he had a delving willingness for attention to detail – the balance which completed the effectiveness of their teamwork.

Moss glanced at his friend, and gave a sour grin. 'Well if Tinemann had been shot, you'd have had a ready-made suspect,' he suggested. 'Our little ornithologist friend Hollis. That automatic he's carrying hardly fits into my rosy picture of a devoted friend of nature's feathered creatures. Blanks or no blanks, that was a nine mil. Beretta.'

Thane nodded, and side-stepped a deep crevice in the rock. 'He says it is licensed, Phil. Still, there's no harm in running a check on the point, or in finding out whether he really was as enthusiastic about Tinemann's ability as a warden as he's trying to make out.'

They had reached a point almost level with the landing place. Looking across the intervening slope of shingle, Moss gave a sudden whistle of surprise.

'Hey, there's another boat down there!'

The new arrival, a small, white-painted speedboat, was tied up alongside Willie MacPherson's antiquated launch. The speedboat, sleek-lined, two powerful outboard engines twin-mounted at its stern, had a tiny, windscreen-shielded cockpit and gleaming chromework. A yacht club pennant hung limp from a midget bowmast.

Thane turned. 'Sergeant –'

Sergeant Stewart hurried forward.

'Recognize the boat?'

The sergeant showed immediate interest. 'Aye, sir.

That'll probably be the doctor come over to have a word with you. He said he'd maybe get a lift out from Mr Sonders.'

'Who's Sonders?' queried Moss. 'Another shark-fisher?'

'Anything but, Inspector.' The uniformed man's voice held a note of disciplined amusement. 'He's a South African, loaded with money by all accounts, but as friendly as they come. That wee speedboat is the tender for his yacht, the *Gabrielle*. Maybe you'd see it as you came out from Inverlay harbour, a big diesel-powered job, painted blue wi' white deckworks.'

They remembered it. Anchored just off the harbour mouth, a deep-draught forty tonner, the *Gabrielle* had had an air of built-in luxury combined with a strength of line and business-like equipment which showed she was no coastal playcraft but an ocean-going vessel of considerable capability.

The *Gabrielle's* boat had been left untended, and obviously its passengers had gone on to the same destination, the warden's hut.

The hut, a small, low-set building made of concrete blocks with a corrugated iron roof, nestled close in under the tower of the automatic light, obviously located there to take advantage of any possible degree of shelter. Some heavy stones placed on the roof as additional ballast told their own story of possible conditions when gales came sweeping in from the surrounding sea. A rainwater barrel stood to one side, and near it an attempt had been made to lay out a miniature garden. Within a boundary of large sea-shells and carefully graded pebbles a handful of marigolds and a scattering of unhappy looking tulips were flowering in a patch of tended but sand-like soil.

Dan Laurence was standing by the doorway, a cigarette loose between his lips. The Scientific Bureau superintendent watched them approach, then jerked his head in the direction of the hut's interior.

'Neat and clean, Colin – except for a scattering of empty

20

bottles under the bed. It's all yours. Oh, and there's a storage shed round at the back, where he kept dried-out driftwood and some other odds and ends. I got one of the local lads to take the pressure stove round there and told him to go ahead with a brew-up. Nothing like tea for lubricating the brain, though it looks as though our bird warden preferred the harder stuff.'

'Whisky?'

'Aye. But not a drop left,' growled Laurence. 'He may have been here only three weeks, but there's a rare pile of empties.

'I've located a few fingerprints here and there, Colin – mostly on the bottles. Once I've eliminated Tinemann's dabs, I'll have a clearer idea how things stand.'

'There's the other angle,' murmured Thane. 'Any dregs of liquor left in these bottles might stand examination.'

The Scientific Bureau superintendent nodded. 'That's in my mind, Colin. Still, the man who could maybe tell you more about that possibility has just arrived.'

'The doctor?' Thane paused in the doorway. 'I saw the motor boat – where is he now?'

'Round the back with the others. He brought a pal with him, and says he's in a hurry to get back to the mainland.'

'Thanks, Dan. I'll have a look around inside the hut, and then see him.'

'That's your department,' said Laurence thankfully. 'Well, it's a nice wee spot this, eh?' He took a deep breath. 'Sea air and sunshine – if we've got to have a murder, Sanctuary Isle's a pleasanter place for it than most.' He took the cigarette from his mouth and gave a bellow. 'Johnny! Time we were moving – there's more work to be done.'

As the summons was answered, Thane went into the hut with Moss close behind him.

'Close the door, Phil.'

It clicked shut, blanketing out the Isle's background chorus of waves and seabirds, and they had their first view

21

of the hut's interior. A one-room structure, sparsely equipped with a bed, folding table and two wooden chairs, some cupboard space along one wall, a sink with hand-operated water pump and, partitioned off in the far corner, a small toilet compartment. A large open fireplace with dead grey ashes in the grate and a pile of driftwood fuel close by completed the basic picture.

Captain Tinemann had obviously been a man of fairly simple needs – despite the cluster of familiarly-shaped bottles. The cupboards and shelves held mainly tinned foodstuffs, a pair of old but powerful binoculars hung behind the door beside a large handtorch, and a battery-powered radio lay on the floor beside one of the chairs.

'Another hobby.' Phil Moss thumbed towards a small, delicately carved wooden book-end, its half-completed companion lying beside it. A similarly carved walking stick lay propped against one wall.

Thane nodded. 'A cosy enough little place.' Springs creaked as he sat down on the bed. 'Cigarette, Phil?'

'Thanks.' Moss took one from the offered packet, accepted a light, and took a deep draw. 'What now?'

'I'm going to have a talk to the doctor, then a session with MacPherson,' said Thane. 'Phil, you concentrate on Hollis. Have a word with Sonders while you're at it. His yacht's been cruising around this area, and that means he's likely to know what boats have been around the Isle lately.' He thudded the flat of one hand against the bed. 'This is a Robinson Crusoe set-up, Phil. The only man on an island gets himself murdered, and so far the nearest witnesses we can locate are twenty thousand ruddy seabirds.'

'He had a pretty lonely life,' mused Moss. 'He couldn't have patrolled this pimple of rock all the hours of the day – and seagulls can't carry on much of a conversation.'

'Wood whittling is a favourite hobby among sailors,' Thane reminded him. 'And he had the radio; there are books lying around, and, from the look of things, a bottle handy. The supply's gone dry . . . maybe that was why he was so anxious for MacPherson to make an extra boat trip.

Well, we'll find out.' He levered himself up from the bed. 'Right, Phil, chase in that doctor.'

His second-in-command departed, and Thane took time to have a closer inspection of the room. Captain Tinemann might have been out of liquor, but his cigarette stock had been adequate. Two large unopened cartons, the same brand as the pack which had been in the dead man's pocket, lay handy in a cupboard beside several tins of beans. His taste in literature had covered a fairly wide range. Thumbing through the main bundle of books, Thane found two paperbacks, a nautical almanac, a tattered volume of Shakespeare and a brightly-jacketed volume which described itself as *A Condensed Historical Guide to the West Highlands*. The final item was a rolled-op Admiralty chart of the Firth of Lorne area, covering the southern tip of Mull, the sea between, Sanctuary Isle, and a stretch of the main Argyll coastline.

There was a quiet knock, and the door opened.

'Chief Inspector Thane? I'm Doctor Connan.'

The medical man came into the hut, closing the door behind him. Freckle-faced, earnest, and still in his late twenties, Doctor Connan was obviously keen to get the interview over.

'I don't want to rush you,' he began. 'But I've got patients to visit, and then an evening surgery –'

'This won't take long,' Thane assured him. 'Thanks for coming over.'

Connan grinned. 'I was lucky. An expectant mother produced exactly on schedule, and then I met Royan Sonders at the quayside. He was just going to return to the *Gabrielle* – that's his yacht –'

Thane nodded. 'I saw it as we came out. A nice-looking boat.'

'Worth fifteen thousand pounds of anybody's money,' agreed Connan enthusiastically. 'Anyway, I've treated a couple of Sonders' crew in the past – cuts, that sort of thing – and when he heard what had happened out here he said he'd take me out himself.' He put one hand into his jacket

23

pocket, produced an envelope, and laid it on the table-top. 'This may save some explanations. I've written up a preliminary report on what I found when I came out to examine Tinemann's body.'

Lifting the envelope, Thane opened it, took out two close-typed sheets of paper, and moved nearer the narrow-framed window before he began reading.

The report was concise, every point clearly indicated, with just sufficient use of the words 'probable' and 'possible' to allow the young medical man room to wriggle clear of cast-iron conclusions.

Connan's eyes twinkled. 'Sorry, Chief Inspector, but I was taught one basic rule when I studied the forensic side of medicine – always leave yourself room to manoeuvre!'

Thane folded the report and returned it to the envelope. 'Words of wisdom,' he acknowledged dryly. 'But you still give the opinion that death was due to aconite poisoning.'

'As certain as I can be until there's a post mortem report to back me up,' declared the freckle-faced doctor. 'I placed the time of death at around eleven last night, based on rigor mortis being complete and with the appropriate fall in body temperature to corroborate. But again I can't be one hundred per cent certain. A night in the open air, especially on an island shore, can upset calculations.'

The situation had to be accepted. Forensic textbooks laid it down that body temperature dropped one degree Centigrade for each hour after death until it reached the temperature of its surroundings. But weather, the exterior temperature, even whether the subject was fat or thin and the type of clothing worn were all factors which had to be considered.

Thane turned to the other, at least equally important point. 'What first made you think he'd been poisoned?'

Young Doctor Connan flushed pink beneath his freckles.

'Well' – he hesitated – 'it was all in the look of the body. Tinemann's face had a blue tinge about it. If he hadn't been out in the open air, with no marks of violence or anything similar, well, I'd probably have said he'd been asphyxiated. It worried me, and I made a closer examination. The whole picture was consistent with poisoning, and the only poison which seemed to match the details was aconite.'

'Now we're getting places,' said Thane brusquely. 'If it doesn't strain you too much, let's assume that it was aconite. Pretty lethal stuff, right?'

'That's right, Chief Inspector. One sixteenth of a grain can be lethal. It's produced from a plant-root which looks very like horse-radish. The best illustration of its strength is that if anyone touched a cut piece of aconite root to his lip for even a second he'd feel his lip go numb.'

'How could it have been given to him?' demanded Thane.

'That's difficult,' confessed Doctor Connan. 'Medically, aconite is seldom used any more, except as a local, purely surface anaesthetic. And even then you've got to be careful. If there's the slightest cut or crack in the patient's skin then aconite is automatically ruled out . . . even when it has been diluted to a fantastic degree.

'It might have been on a cigarette or – or' – he caught a glimpse of the empty bottles – 'or in a drink of some kind. It's soluble in alcohol.'

'Uh-huh.' Thane had become more friendly. 'Supposing it was in whisky. How long before it would act?'

'That depends' – the young man chewed his upper lip. 'I've given you a rough estimate of time of death. But the poison itself could have been administered one to eight hours before. Aconite hits different people different ways, though the first effects would be felt fairly quickly. After about fifteen minutes he'd have a stomach pain, gradually worsening. By the time he really became worried, it would be really acting. One side-effect is spreading paralysis and finally a complete numbness.'

Thane frowned. 'Pretty nasty. You mean he'd be staggering around out there for quite a spell, just going around in circles?'

Connan shook his head. 'No. Didn't anyone tell you, Chief Inspector? There's an emergency beacon of drift-wood down at the south end of the Isle. If it was lit, the blaze could be seen from the mainland – and that's the recognized distress signal. A boat would have come out from Inverlay. Captain Tinemann must have been trying to get to the beacon, but the aconite caught up with him first. It wouldn't affect the brain – he'd be conscious and clear-headed to the last. But he'd just have to lie there until it was his time to die.'

Thane flicked the end of his cigarette into the wood-ash of the fireplace. 'One last thing, Doctor Connan. Supposing Willie MacPherson hadn't made that unscheduled run to the Isle this morning. Supposing it had been another couple of days before anyone went out there and found him. If there had been that kind of time-lapse, would you still have said he'd been poisoned?'

The doctor was silent for several seconds, deliberately avoiding Thane's steady gaze. At last he looked up. 'I'll be honest, Chief Inspector. By that time, the main signs would have gone. If I had found a retired sea captain dead on an island, with no apparent signs of injury and lying as if he'd had a minor fall, then I'd probably have written it off as heart failure due to shock, and made out a death certificate on the spot.'

'Thanks.' Thane said the word softly. 'That's probably the way it was intended to be. Right, doctor, you can get back to those patients now. You won't be involved in the post mortem, but I'll let you know the results. Oh, and doctor – ask MacPherson to come in next, will you?'

Connan nodded, then stopped, one hand on the door. 'Chief Inspector – it's not my province, but, well, you may find him untalkative. Willie's all right, it's just that he's had a brush or two with the law in the past.'

'So I gathered,' said Thane ruefully, remembering the pitching boat-trip across the Firth. 'What was it? Poaching?'

'Nope.' Connan grinned, relaxed now that his part in the

26

proceedings was over. 'Willie runs – ran, I mean – the best illicit still in the county. You might call the result bootleg liquor, but it goes down the throat like the kiss of mountain dew. Ask the sergeant, and he'll tell you how good it is – but leave that until Inspector Davidson's not around.'

He gave a wink, opened the door, and went out. Thane picked up the typewritten report from the table, put it in his pocket, then went over to the window and looked out. Once or twice during his talk with Connan he'd been sure he had heard a distant sound which might have been Hollis, the Bird Society convenor, firing off more blank cartridges from his pistol. But Hollis was standing only a few feet away, talking earnestly to Phil Moss. Beyond them he could see the landing place and the two boats still tied side by side.

The sound came again, this time a definite but far-off gunshot. He saw Hollis break off his conversation and point out to sea, disapproval written large across his face. Phil Moss gave a nod and said something in reply, but whatever the object of their attention, it was beyond the window's tight line of vision.

The hut door opened and he turned. Reluctance in his step, a light of caution in his eyes, Willie MacPherson entered the room. The boatman had formed his own shrewd opinion of Thane on the sea journey from the mainland, and had decided that the next few minutes were most definitely marked 'handle with care.' He let the door click quietly shut behind him, and stood waiting.

'Sit down, Willie,' invited Thane. 'What's going on out there?'

'Och, it's Mr Hollis complaining again,' replied the boatman, taking a chair. 'He's moaning about Finn Preston being so near to the Isle.'

'The shark-hunter?' Thane was immediately interested.

'Aye, except he's chasing seals at the moment. Maybe the ones you saw leaving the Isle as we came in. Preston's boat is prowling out there less than a mile off shore. Didn't you hear his rifle at work?'

Thane nodded. 'And Mr Hollis doesn't approve?'

'That's a mild way of putting it.' MacPherson let a faint smile linger on his face. 'But as long as Preston's shooting the seals at sea, there's not a thing Hollis can do about it. And Preston won't stop – it's part of the way he makes his living.'

'Just another job of work to him.' Thane lifted the other chair, swung it round so that its wooden back faced the boat-man, then sat saddle-fashion with his arms resting on the chair-back. 'Well, while we're on the subject of how people earn a living, maybe we'd better get one thing clear. I'm only interested in Captain Tinemann's death. I'm not an Argyll County officer. If I come across a witness who, for example, might be running a do-it-yourself whisky still in his back yard it doesn't concern me – as long as he tells me all he knows about the murder. Understand, Willie?'

The boatman shifted awkwardly in his chair. 'What if the story was a bit awkward to explain without this witness o' yours maybe getting into a wee spot of bother?'

'Then I'd make a point of making sure that the "wee spot of bother" was ignored for once.' Thane took his cigarettes from his pocket. 'Smoke?'

The boatman shook his head. 'It is not good for the palate – or the wind, come to that. All right, Chief Inspector, I'll take your word about standing between me and that bit of bother. What is it you want?'

'Your version of what happened, starting with yesterday, when you brought these supplies out to Tinemann. And Willie' – Thane rubbed a thumb along his chin – 'let's forget the story about fuel-oil spoiling some of the food. There's enough stuff in this hut to keep two people for a week.'

Willie MacPherson took it without a blush. 'Och well, it was just the first thing I could think to say,' he admitted. 'You'll need to understand, the captain was a grand old fellow, always ready for a yarn and fond of a bit dram of the hard stuff. Not a one for soaking up his liquor – but just liking a glass or two now and again, and maybe a few more if he was entertaining company. And mind, it can be dam' lonely out here with nothing but these birds for company.'

'So you used to bring him out a weekly bottle or two along with the Bird Society supplies,' suggested Thane.

The boatman agreed. 'Six bottles a week – he was religiously inclined, you see, not given to drinking on the Sabbath.'

Thane suppressed a chuckle. 'A pretty expensive pastime for a man drawing retirement pension,' he commented. 'And I don't suppose he was drawing a particularly large pay-packet from the Bird Society.'

'He told me he got five pounds a week and free supplies,' said MacPherson. 'Of course, they wouldn't have been classing the whisky in that.' He hesitated, then probed cautiously, 'It's a terrible business, the amount of tax on a bottle of whisky – and it a decent old man's pleasure.'

Thane lent a hand. 'But if the captain managed to get his bottles without having to worry about such things as tax, then the man concerned would be doing a friendly thing.'

'Ah' – the boatman beamed agreement. 'Just so. Only I wasn't able to bring even a bottle out yesterday, due to a wedding up Oban way and the bride my mother's cousin's daughter. The captain was a bit put out, what with having taken the last dram he had before breakfast that day. So I said I'd make another trip out this morning – and the rest you know, except here's me got to go and report finding a body, and six bottles of the best triple-run stuff lying in the boat!'

'Awkward,' agreed Thane.

The boatman gave a deep sigh. 'I had to put them over the side on the trip back to Inverlay. Six bottles at the bottom of the Firth . . . och, a terrible waste.'

Thane stood up and looked out of the window. Hollis had left, and Phil Moss was now deep in earnest conversation with a stranger, a sharp-eyed but somewhat paunchy individual wearing a yachting cap, open-necked white shirt and bleached linen trousers, the latter held at the waist by a heavy black leather belt. Over one arm he carried what looked like a waterproof duffel jacket. Royan Sonders, guessed Thane. Otherwise, the island scene was unchanged. If Finn Preston's boat was still in the area, it remained out of view of the window.

'Willie, did you tell anyone that you'd have to make a second trip out to the Isle today?'

'No.' There was no hesitation in the boatman's reply. 'Not a soul, sir. I keep my business to myself.'

'Take a look at these bottles,' requested Thane. 'Any of them yours?'

MacPherson went over to the pile – and inspected each bottle in turn. 'Just these two with the square-sided shape,' he declared. 'The captain brought them over with him, before we made our . . . arrangement.' He glanced at his watch. 'Eh, when are we likely to be heading back, Chief Inspector?'

'First the doctor and now you,' growled Thane. 'What's the rush?'

The boatman appeared a trifle embarrassed. 'The other lads in the band are expecting me over about seven. It's coming up for six o'clock now.'

'Another sideline?' queried Thane. 'I'd have said that running a motor launch and a whisky still would have kept you going.'

'Och well, the boat's only needed now and again,' explained MacPherson. 'Maybe with the odd party of holidaymakers who want to go cruising or fishing. And the – the other thing – is looked after by my mother's cousin's son. So sometimes during the day I put on my kilt and play the bagpipes for the visitors, who usually have a bit spare silver. Then at night I play at the local dances.' With some pride, he added, 'We've got our own band in Inverlay, the South Lorne Stompers. . . . I play clarinet.'

'In the kilt?' queried Thane.

30

The boatman blinked. 'In evening dress, Mr Thane. The dances are not for the tourists.'

Thane sought safer ground. 'The Bird Society always used your boat to ferry their members out to the island. Any way of checking who was in these groups?'

MacPherson nodded, strode over to one of the shelves, moved some tinned food aside, and produced a large leather-bound book. 'They'll all be in here. Every visitor had to sign the book and give his home address. Captain Tinemann was most particular about it.'

'No exceptions?'

'Well . . .' the boatman shrugged. 'He wouldn't be bothering if it was a friend who sailed in for a talk and a dram. Myself, now, I wouldn't have to bother. Nor would Finn Preston.'

'Preston landed here?' The shark-hunter's activities seemed slowly but surely to be growing in their importance to the bird warden's death. Thane stared hard at the boatman. 'Are you sure? I thought the Bird Society didn't like him.'

MacPherson scratched behind one ear. 'They don't. But he and Captain Tinemann got on all right – at least, he used to moor off shore a bit and come in by dinghy for a drink and a blether. I think the old captain was out at Preston's boat a couple of times – but then, he wouldn't want Mr Hollis or the Bird Society to know about that.'

Thane tapped the chair-back with one suddenly demanding forefinger. 'Willie, was Preston's boat anywhere near the island yesterday?'

'Not when I was out,' answered the boatman. Then, slowly, almost reluctantly, he added, 'But when I told Captain Tinemann that he'd have to wait until the next day for the whisky, he wasn't too concerned. He said Finn Preston would probably be calling at the Isle some time that afternoon.'

Thane was silent, digesting the surprise information. Then he strode across the room until he stood close beside the smaller man. 'All right, Willie. That's all for now –

31

except that I don't want you talking about this to anyone back at Inverlay. Understood?'

The man nodded.

'Oh, and one last point, Willie. Did the captain write many letters, or receive any mail?'

'Nothing worth talking about either way, Chief Inspector. Eh, let's think now – I posted a couple of letters for him once, both addressed to places abroad, to friends he'd made when at sea, he told me. Then there was another, to some shop down in London. As far as mail arriving was concerned, I took out only one letter. It was an official-looking thing, something to do with his pension if I remember rightly.'

It was as Thane had imagined. Captain Tinemann, a sailor too old for the sea, had had few real ties with life on land. As a result, he'd probably found little unusual in the island's solitude, might even have welcomed it.

He followed MacPherson out of the hut, and collided with Phil Moss, who had been about to enter.

Moss's thin features held an expression of considerable satisfaction as he gestured the man at his side to come closer. 'Mr Sonders, this is Chief Inspector Thane. I think he'd like to hear what you've been telling me.'

Royan Sonders smiled, showing a gold-crowned flash among an otherwise perfect dental display. 'If it helps, you're welcome.'

They shook hands. 'You own the *Gabrielle*, don't you?' said Thane. 'I saw her outside Inverlay harbour – a fine-looking boat.'

Sonders was pleased by the compliment. 'Happy to show you over her any time, Chief Inspector,' he declared. 'You too, Inspector Moss – you'll find she's even better seen at close range.'

'We might do that,' agreed Thane. On initial impression, he was finding it just a little difficult to tag Sonders into a definite category. The man was just about the right age to have been involved in World War Two – and probably, he guessed, had made at least part of his money in the general post-war scramble. The South African had the competent, driving air of a man who didn't wait for opportunity to knock on his door but who went out and dragged it in by the scruff of the neck. Accent carefully neutral, manner polite, Royan Sonders was no soft-living playboy. 'Being in these waters makes you a long way from home, Mr Sonders.'

The yacht owner nodded. 'I'm from Johannesburg originally, Chief Inspector. But I've been in Europe for a long time now – most of my business is based on Switzerland, around Lucerne. Nice enough country around there, but I prefer a sea-coast – and this part of the world takes a lot of beating.' One hand made an apologetic gesture. 'Sorry, I'm going off the track a little, and you're busy. Well, where do I start? Inspector Moss gave me quite a grilling.'

Moss gave a faint cough. 'Just routine, as I told you, Mr Sonders. But you'll remember I asked you about yesterday, and whether the *Gabrielle* had been at her moorings.'

Sonders grew serious. 'Yesterday, when the bird warden was killed. No, we sailed from Inverlay about ten a.m. At first, we cruised among the smaller islands to the south, pottering around more than anything – exploring in comfort, and without any rush.

'Anyway, it was early evening before we turned back, and the return trip was considerably slower. I was taking it easy and, anyway, there was a mist gathering which meant I didn't feel like taking chances. I think it would be about seven p.m. when I saw Preston's boat. . . .'

'Where?' Thane snapped the word.

Sonders frowned. 'That's what Inspector Moss wanted to know. But it's difficult – there was a mist, with visibility down to maybe half a mile. The *Gabrielle* was heading in towards Inverlay, and Preston's boat was in the distance, coming down the Firth from the north. It was his boat, but I've seen it around so often since I came here that I just didn't pay much attention.'

'Could he have been heading towards Sanctuary Isle?'

'Maybe – maybe not.' The South African shrugged. 'I'm sorry, Chief Inspector. It wasn't important at the time.'

'It still helps, Mr Sonders,' said Thane. 'It may help more than you think.'

'Well, I'm glad. And now, I promised Doctor Connan –'

'He told me, he wants to get back,' nodded Thane. 'If you're ready to take him to the mainland again, I've no other questions for now.'

Sonders said goodbye, and began the scramble over the rocks to the landing place. Doctor Connan was already there, they got aboard the speedboat, and moments later its twin outboards barked to life. The boat moved gently at first, feeling its way out of the narrow channel. Then the engine noise increased, a broad white wake began creaming from the little craft's stern as it headed out into the open water beyond, skimming and bumping over the wave-crests on a fast course back to the mainland.

'We'll be out there again soon,' said Moss grimly. He took a cardboard pillbox from one pocket, shook two small pellets on to the palm of his hand, and then swallowed them. The performance wasn't over. From his handkerchief pocket he carefully fished a small twist of paper, extracted two considerably larger pills, jet black and marble-shaped, and took them one after the other in quick succession.

'The black ones are new,' commented Thane, mildly interested.

His companion agreed. 'Activated charcoal,' he explained with sober clinical concern. 'I'm trying it out along with the regular pills – they're magnesium oxide. The oxide neutralizes the stomach acids and the charcoal soothes. At least, that's the theory.'

Thane gave a heartless grin. 'You'd have been better investing in some anti-seasickness tablets.'

# Chapter Two

What hotel accommodation there was in the village of Inverlay would hardly have qualified for inclusion in any five-star listings. But the Inverlay Arms, a snug old-fashioned two-storey building with thick walls of grey native stone, had a friendly staff, clean and comfortable beds, and a dining room window which gazed out across the fishing village's small but busy harbour.

Colin Thane spread a thick coating of farm butter on another piece of toast, contemplated the plate of bacon and eggs which had just been placed before him by an apple-cheeked young waitress, and prepared to enjoy breakfast. Across the table, Phil Moss added first sugar then salt to the steaming bowl of porridge before him, poured some milk over the result, and stifled a half-formed yawn. The time was 8 a.m., much of Inverlay was obviously up and busy – but then, the vast majority of the village's solid Highland citizenry made a habit of retiring for the night about ten, and it had been nearer 3 a.m. before the two detectives had been able to try to make up some part of their sleep quota. By that time they'd demolished the bulk of immediate inquiries, and Dan Laurence had returned to the city in a car loaded with items from the Isle which required detailed examination in the Scientific Bureau laboratories.

Thane chewed a first forkful of bacon, and found it was excellent. The dining-room was still quiet; a lone commercial traveller had just finished his meal and departed, the only other hotel guests who had made an appearance, a young and obviously honeymooning couple, were at a corner table.

He tackled the nearest egg on his plate. As the yolk cut, oozing a rich yellow, Phil Moss gave a grunt. 'That reminds me – when should we get the p.m. report on Tinemann?'

'Must you?' Thane lowered his fork and grimaced. 'You miserable – ach, they told us we'd get the result some time this morning. Why? What's worrying you?'

Moss frowned. 'Everybody seems sure Tinemann died from aconite poisoning – yet at the same time, the medical characters agree that Tinemann would be alive for at least an hour. Why couldn't he get to that emergency beacon and get it lit?'

'It puzzles me too,' admitted Thane. 'Remember, though, aconite can hit different people different ways. In Tinemann's case the paralysis effect may have occurred quickly – and severely.'

As an explanation it didn't particularly satisfy either of them – but it was only one of a number of points which still had to be looked into, points which might mean little or nothing yet which still had to be explored in detail. Their late-night slog, using as a temporary office the solitary, unoccupied cell in Inverlay's cottage-sized police station, had brought matters only a little further forward.

First, there had been the inevitable formalities of signed statements. One from Edgar Hollis, the Bird Society committee convenor who at the same time had produced the permit for his Beretta automatic; another from Willie MacPherson, still apprehensive at the possibility of the limelight being turned on some of his activities; a third from Royan Sonders.

Two of Sonders' all-French crew of four aboard the *Gabrielle* backed the South African's story of seeing Finn Preston's boat near Sanctuary Isle on the evening of the murder. The other two said they'd been below deck at the relevant time.

Other facts matched up. At the harbour, fishermen

36

agreed that there had been a thin, obscuring sea-mist over part of tile Firth of Lorne that evening, a mist which finally cleared about an hour before dusk. The *Gabrielle* had been seen to anchor just outside the harbour entrance at a time which corresponded with Sonders' story of his return. Finn Preston's boat, while known to be around the Firth area, hadn't put into port until sometime the following morning.

The porridge plate empty, Phil Moss pushed it to one side, contemplated the toast, and settled for tea and a cigarette.

'Here's another point,' he said. 'Preston looks like being our man, but why does Hollis say he didn't know Captain Tinemann was a bottle-a-day man?'

'No reason why it shouldn't be true,' shrugged Thane. 'Some of these old Merchant Navy characters can absorb that amount of liquor – even backwoods snakejuice – without turning a hair. But the old captain wouldn't broadcast the fact. He probably felt that his new employers might take the view that birds and booze don't mix. You checked the bird sanctuary visitors book – it showed that Tinemann was on his own most of the time, with no-one to peer over his shoulder.'

His companion gave a nod of agreement. 'He'd been out there for three weeks. If you discount MacPherson's supply runs, then there were only six official visits – three of those Bird Society parties, another a boat-load of school-children, one by Royan Sonders and a party from his yacht, and' – Moss gave a faint grin – 'we mustn't forget the Inverlay branch outing of the Women's Temperance Guild.'

'Complete with Captain Tinemann chewing pepper-mints.' Thane said it without malice. The murdered bird warden, whatever his weaknesses, seemed from all accounts to have been a friendly, likeable individual. Over-night, the earlier inquiries set in motion by Argyll police had traced the dead man's only living relative, an elderly sister who lived in a cottage on the outskirts of Southport.

Apart from that one kinswoman, the retired sailor had no ties on land – though the shipping line which paid him a monthly pension spoke of him as having many friends afloat. 'You know, Phil, it would be a major help if we had some idea about the possible motive. When it comes to poisoning, there's generally stronger than usual motive behind the killing. . . .'

He broke off. The honeymoon couple, hand-in-hand on their way out of the dining room, had become entangled with the blue-uniformed figure of Inspector Davidson. The county officer finally brushed them aside and strode across the room.

''Morning, sir.' He beamed down at Thane. 'I've got some news that should interest you – Finn Preston's boat is back in harbour. It tied up about half an hour ago.'

Thane looked out at the harbour with fresh interest. 'Which one is his?'

Davidson pointed. 'The red-hulled motor sailer tied up near the harbour entrance. Preston calls her the *Rock Rose*.' Even at that distance, the shark-fisher's boat was obviously of a different breed from the others she lay alongside. Smaller, blunt-bowed, broad of beam, her clinker-built hull giving a low freeboard, this was a craft with an air of rugged, unglamorous purpose. But, for the moment, she rested. Her for'ard mounted harpoon gun was covered by canvas, some newly washed shirts were draped to dry over the upturned dinghy mounted aft, her deck appeared deserted. The mast set just to the rear of the wheelhouse had its boom lashed down, sails tightly furled.

'I'm going to pay Preston a visit,' said Thane. 'But sit down, man –' He waited until the county officer had dragged over another chair. 'Any sign of the post mortem report?'

Davidson flushed. 'Sorry, Chief Inspector. I've got it with me. I was bringing it over when I heard about Preston.' He unbuttoned the top right-hand pocket of his tunic and handed over the envelope. Thane slit the gummed-down flap with his toast knife and took out the carbon copy report – by now, the original was probably on its way to the Procurator Fiscal, the Scottish law officer who, at the end of the day, would have the responsibility of assembling any prosecution case for the courts.

Cigarette in one corner of his mouth, Thane scanned the document. Professor MacMaster, the tall, gaunt forensic expert from Glasgow University, had been the principal pathologist at the post mortem.

For MacMaster that had meant the long journey from the city to Oban and then a grim mortuary session which had lasted until long after midnight. The thin, humourless professor was no longer young – but Thane would have been surprised to have seen any other name attached to the post mortem findings. Legend in medical school had it that old MacMaster spent his summer holidays patrolling the beach of his favourite resort on the off-chance that a body might be washed ashore. Unkind, but a not unfaithful reflection of the detached professional delight with which he swooped on anything interesting in the shape of sudden or unusual death.

'The body was that of . . .' Colin Thane read through the emotionless antiseptic phrasings which summed up condition of internal organs and brain tissue, general physique and other factors which had to be listed to establish that, from a medical point of view, the dead bird warden had been a healthy specimen, not in any way due for natural death.

Then, and only then, did MacMaster's report get down to forensic fact.

'While there were indications that death occurred some hours after the subject's last meal, a considerable quantity of alcohol was present in the stomach and appeared to have been consumed perhaps two hours before death. Examination of the proportion of alcohol in the blood confirmed the view that the subject would have appeared to be in a condition which, to use a handy illustration, might have resulted in his being regarded as technically

39

unfit to drive a motor vehicle. Death was due to the action of aconite (aconitine, aconitum lycoctonum) on the respiratory system, resulting in a paralytic action on the respiratory centre. A considerable quantity of aconite was present in the organs and in the alcohol referred to previously. There were no signs of external violence or hypodermic puncture marks. My conclusion is that the aconite poison was in all probability contained in the alcohol, and was the sole cause of death.'

Thane folded the report sheet, stubbed his cigarette, and rose from his chair. 'Phil, a couple of things. I want coastguard stations and lighthouses within a twenty – no, make it a thirty mile radius contacted with a request that they list all remembered sightings of vessels throughout the afternoon and evening of the murder. It'll probably be pretty scrappy, but it may help plug another leak in the kettle.'

'I can guess the second job,' said Moss. 'To keep tabs on the aconite sources, check round chemists and doctors.'

'Right,' agreed Thane. 'It isn't likely to do much good, but it is necessary. And I'm interested in making another trip out to Sanctuary Isle. Get hold of Willie MacPherson, and tell him he's got a booking in an hour's time.'

There, at least, the Argyll officer could give some positive help. 'I've already asked MacPherson to stand by,' he told them. 'The two men left on guard at the Isle have to be relieved this morning.'

'Fine.' Thane looked out of the window again, across the harbour. 'Well, I'll see you later. I'm going over to the *Rock Rose*, and if Finn Preston is aboard he should be able to clear up one or two angles.'

'Should,' murmured Phil Moss. 'But will he?'

Should, maybe could, but would he? Thane left the hotel, went out into the warm sunshine, and headed across the roadway. He rounded a small mountain of empty fish crates, and walked on down the cement length of the harbour quay. Some of the fishing boats were preparing for sea, diesel engines puttering softly while their crews finished a last round of tasks. Aboard one weather-stained

40

drift net boat, a youngster sat by the stern peeling potatoes and listening to a transistor radio pulsing a multi-guitar rhythm.

Salt air, an occasional waft of stinking fish offal, greedy, raucous gulls and the blue-cloud of diesel oil merged into a surprisingly pleasant, almost relaxed atmosphere. But Thane kept his eyes flexed on the motor sailer ahead. A wisp of smoke was coming from the small stove-pipe chimney set aft of the wheelhouse, and from somewhere within the vessel he could hear the muted clanking of metal.

He stopped beside the *Rock Rose*, glanced round again, then jumped the two foot distance to her deck. As his feet hit the wood, the clanking stopped.

'Finn? Is that you?' It was a girl's voice, and the tone was one of exasperation. Thane moved forward, into the compact wheelhouse, and then, lowering his head, made his way down the half dozen rungs of the wooden-slatted companionway ladder leading to the cabin.

'Finn . . . this thing's jammed again!' Inside the small cabin one of the deck panels had been removed. A small but unmistakenly feminine figure was bent over the dark space, her back towards him, the seat of her oilstained blue jeans strained at the seams, one arm supporting her, the other lost from sight. 'Finn' – the girl's head turned, and she gave a sudden frown.

'Hello.' Thane gave a friendly grin.

'Who the devil are you?' The girl wriggled round, sitting on the deck and subjecting her visitor to a frank, critical inspection. Between twenty and twenty-five, he guessed. Her hair crammed beneath an old scarf, tied turban fashion, and a heavy jersey which was several sizes too large didn't quite manage to disguise the slim, firmly rounded body beneath its loose folds. 'Where's Finn?'

'I'm Chief Inspector Thane, and I don't know where he is.' Thane squatted down beside the girl and peered into the gloom of the boat's bilge-space. 'Having trouble?'

She gave him a glare. 'No – I enjoy mending bilge-

41

pumps. It's my hobby. Know anything about them?' An attractive enough girl, even in her present, hardly flattering rig. Dark-eyed, brunette, with a nose and mouth which, separately, might each have been termed a little too large by Hollywood standards but which combined to give her face a warm strength of character, she sat back and gave an expressive grimace.

'No – bilge-pumps don't come into the police training manual,' confessed Thane. 'Is it serious?'

'Only if you can't swim.' The girl picked up a hank of clean waste rag lying beside her, wiped her hands on it, and then inspected the result. 'Smooth velvet hands – huh, mine are more like sandpaper. I've kept telling him to rig a mechanical pump instead of using these ancient levers. Noah probably picked them up second-hand for the Ark.' She paused for breath, then added, 'I'm Gwen Preston.'

'His sister?'

'No, wife. Which also means cook, deckhand, cabin-boy, second engineer, business manager and general dogsbody.' For the first time he noticed the thin gold wedding ring. 'Well, Chief Inspector, you and Finn seem to be chasing one another. He went ashore about ten minutes ago, intending to make a telephone call and then take a walk round to see you. Is it true what they're saying about Captain Tinemann – that he's been murdered?'

'It's true,' nodded Thane. 'That's why I'm here. Your husband knew the captain, I'm told. . . .'

'Knew him?' Gwen Preston gave a laugh. 'When Finn went over to see the old rogue there was no saying when he'd come back. Captain Tinemann kept open house as far as Finn was concerned.'

'Had he known your husband before he took on the job of bird warden?' Thane stood up and promptly banged his head on the cabin roof.

'Everybody does that at first.' The girl also rose to her feet, She was small, her head hardly level with his shoulder. 'Yes, they knew each other. Finn was a merchant navy apprentice, still in his teens, during the last war. He was on

42

Captain Tinemann's ship when it was torpedoed in the North Atlantic. They were in the same lifeboat for three days before they were picked up.' She looked at him again, suddenly cautious. 'Why? What's all this got to do with the captain being killed?'

Thane was saved the trouble of replying. Feet landed lightly on the deck above, steps moved towards the wheelhouse, and then the cabin was darkened as Finn Preston squeezed down the companionway ladder.

Take the popular conception of a giant, bearded Norse Viking, put him into modern dress – in this case an open-necked Government surplus khaki shirt and old corduroy slacks, feet in worn leather sandals – give your Viking a thick, neat-trimmed gold-bronze beard, curly-haired chest and massive muscular build, and you saw Finn Preston. He had to stoop low in the cabin, but he did it with an ease born of long practice. Even alongside Colin Thane's not inconsiderable height and bulk the shark-fisher dominated the cabin's space. This, decided Thane, was not the size of man you willingly tackled in a fight – unless, of course, you had a nice hefty baton in your hand and could keep out of his road long enough to use it! He had a brief, outrageous vision of Preston in bare-knuckle combat with a shark, and felt vaguely sorry for the fish.

'Chief Inspector Thane?' Preston extended one brawny hand. 'They told me at the hotel you'd come down this way. I must have missed you by a few seconds.'

A certain glint in the shark-fisher's grey-blue eyes put Thane on guard. His hand went out, too, but as their grips met he clasped high and equally hard. Preston's smile didn't change, but the grip increased its vice-like hold. Thane appeared equally unnoticing of anything out of the ordinary – then, at last, just before his hand reached the point of loosing its counter grip and giving in like so much jellied veal, the pressure slackened.

The shark-fisher gave a deep-throated chuckle. 'Call it a draw,' he offered.

43

'And welcome,' agreed Thane while he massaged his fingers.

Gwen Preston sighed. 'That, I'm afraid, is an example of my husband's alleged sense of humour, Mr Thane. Finn, the bilge-pump has seized again.'

'I'll fix it,' said Preston casually. 'Like a drink, Chief Inspector?' He had already opened one of the cabin lockers, bringing out two glasses and a large, dark but unlabelled bottle.

'Never before 9 a.m.,' declined Thane.

Preston shrugged, allowed a full three fingers of the liquor to gurgle into one of the glasses, and glanced questioningly towards his wife. She shook her head, and he corked the bottle, picked up his glass, and took a long gulp.

'Ahh.' He wiped his mouth with the back of one hand. 'Yes, I was looking for you, Chief Inspector.'

'And he for you, Finn,' emphasized his wife sharply.

'I'd guessed that,' growled Preston. 'All right, Chief Inspector, let me get my question in first. I was a friend of old Tinemann. I know you've been asking people how often I visited the Isle. Why?'

'We call it routine,' said Thane. 'But I'd like to talk to you – alone.'

The shark-fisher raised one bushy eyebrow, then nodded. 'Gwen, away into the galley and wash the breakfast dishes. We'll go up to the wheelhouse.'

Gwen Preston didn't like the idea. 'My dishes are washed – and the only breakfast you've had is that glass in your hand.'

Preston gave a rumble. 'Then go and make some, woman – stop arguing. You promised to love, honour and obey. Let's see a bit of obeying from you.'

The girl's eyes flashed fire for a moment, then she shrugged and went towards the stern. A moment later a loud clatter of metal came from the direction of the galley, Preston winced.

44

'That was the kettle.' He finished his drink at a gulp, and put the glass down. 'Let's go up.'

Thane followed him back up the companionway to the wheelhouse. It was laid out in compact style, steering wheel and engine controls, compass binnacle and other instruments set out in ideal style to allow one man to control all without having to move from his central position. To one side was a gun-rack, two heavy rifles and a pump-action shot-gun in its mounts and each chained secure through the trigger guard.

Preston turned and slid shut the hatchway covering the cabin entrance. When he faced Thane again, the tanned, bearded face had lost its smile and the grey-blue eyes were suddenly serious.

'Now we can talk. Gwen and I share most things, Chief Inspector . . . but I bumped into Willie MacPherson on my way back after trying to find you at the Inverlay Arms. If what he tells me is right, then let's leave my wife out of this.'

'Suits me.' Thane was trying hard to make up his mind about the rough, bearded giant, and finding it no easy task. There was a hard self-reliance in the man, a salt-etched confidence and yet a concern which was obviously impersonal. 'You came looking for me. Why?'

'Because of old Tinemann, like I said.' Preston gave a growl. 'I served under him when I was a kid.'

'Your wife told me,' agreed Thane. 'Cigarette?'

Finn Preston glanced at the packet and shook his head. 'I stick to filter-tips.' As Thane lit a cigarette for himself, the shark-fisher leaned back against a timber strut. 'When I sailed with Tinemann I rated him the blackest-hearted old basket that had ever held a captain's ticket. When we were torpedoed I jumped into the nearest lifeboat – and cursed my luck when we picked him out of the water. He ran that lifeboat as if he had a twenty-foot bull whip in one hand, had us doing P.T. in mid-Atlantic with the temperature below freezing. But we were all alive when we were picked up.'

45

'Did you know he was coming up to the bird sanctuary?' Thane let the smoke trickle from his nostrils and watched it drift blue across a patch of sunlight.

Preston frowned. 'No. But I heard his name once he'd gone out to the Isle, and decided to take a trip out to see if it was the same man. After that, I got into the habit of going out two, maybe three tides a week.' One huge hand gripped the compass binnacle, almost covering its face. 'And that's it. Willie the boatman says he told you I was due to go out to Sanctuary Isle the evening the captain was killed. And Willie also said he had heard a version of what you'd been told by Sonders.' He pronounced the name as if it were an objectionable smell. 'It seems our gold-toothed yachtsman and some of the *Gabrielle's* crew say they saw my boat heading out towards the Isle.'

'Well, were they right?' asked Thane.

'Yes and no.' Preston chewed his lip. 'That's part of what I was on my way to see you about. I'd told old Tinemann I'd probably come over that evening unless I spotted that he had company . . . the Bird Society doesn't rate me a particularly desirable visitor. Anyway, I was steering down-Firth towards the Isle when I spotted a pair of basking sharks, twenty-five footers if they were an inch. Sharks mean money, Chief Inspector. The bigger the shark, the bigger the money – so I veered off course and chased the things almost across to Mull.'

'You mean you caught the sharks but didn't go to Sanctuary Isle? Who was with you on the *Rock Rose*? Your wife?' True or false, the story was handy but could hardly be described as either strong or convincing.

For the first time, Preston appeared a trifle embarrassed. 'I was on my own in the boat and I didn't get the sharks – but I didn't go to the Isle.' He glanced round at the closed hatch cover and gave a sigh. 'I could use another drink – ach, but maybe it wouldn't be wise. Gwen would come popping up like a jack-in-the-box, wanting to know what was going on. Look, Chief Inspector, do you know anything about catching sharks?'

'Only the two-legged variety,' said Thane mildly. 'But I'm interested.'

'We go after baskers,' said Preston. 'The largest fish in the North Atlantic, bar none – up to thirty feet long, a minimum of five tons in weight when they're full grown. We're free-lance fishers, selling to the highest buyer – and it's the shark liver they're after, maybe a ton of it per fish. When prices are good, that means £50 to £100 a catch. But it's at very least a two of a crew job the way the *Rock Rose* operates – one on the harpoon gun, the other at the wheel.

'Going after these two big 'uns on my own was pretty crazy – I'd sailed the *Rock Rose* up to Oban in the early afternoon and left Gwen ashore there. She was visiting a girl friend, and staying overnight with her. Anyway, after about half an hour of a chase after these sharks, I fired one shot, missed, chased around through the mist for a couple of hours and then gave up. By then, it would be about nine o'clock, and the boat was a good five miles off the west coast of Mull.'

'But you could still have got back to the Isle,' prodded Thane.

The big shark-fisher tugged his beard and agreed. He'd simply decided not to bother, he claimed. Instead, he had sailed the *Rock Rose* in towards Mull, had anchored in a sheltered cove, and spent the night aboard the boat. Next morning he sailed up to Oban, collected his wife at the quay, refuelled, and then they'd gone out after seals.

'I've an agreement with the salmon netters. The seals have been damaging their gear and scaring the fish – so I get so much per seal killed and carcase produced.'

'I heard you operating off the Isle yesterday,' nodded Thane. 'You still didn't know about Tinemann?'

'No.' Preston flushed. 'You're coming perilous close to calling me a liar, Chief Inspector. I've told you before, the Bird Society don't like me – they don't like hunters in any form. Sanctuary Isle is a seal breeding ground, and they

47

can block me from going ashore. But if I shoot seals in the Firth they can't do a thing.

'I thought of looking in on old Tinemann – but when I saw Willie MacPherson's launch at the landing place I guessed the captain had visitors and stayed clear. Gwen and I only sailed into Inverlay this morning, and that's the first I knew about it.' The blue-grey eyes narrowed. 'What about Sonders? Didn't he tell you he saw me veer off after the sharks?'

Thane shook his head. 'He simply remembers seeing you in the area. You don't like him very much, do you?'

The other man swore. 'He must have seen me, mist or no mist. Conditions weren't as bad as all that, and I cut across his ruddy bow – less than a hundred and fifty yards ahead of his floating gin-hulk. No, I don't like him – that's an understatement. He used to moor the *Gabrielle* in the harbour, and I berthed alongside. Then he said he'd rather moor outside, that he found the smell disagreeable. All right, maybe there's a bit of a stink from the fish-hold at times – when you're carrying half of a shark's guts around that's inevitable. But we scrub every foot of deck-space almost daily. Did you notice any smell?'

Thane hadn't, and he said so.

'Right, because she's clean. But that pot-bellied fool first of all tried to get me tossed out of my berth because the *Rock Rose* was "insanitary". And I'll tell you another thing, policeman. It might do you no harm to find out a bit more about Sonders – such as whether he couldn't have been the one who landed on the Isle.' By now, Preston's face was flushed red.

Was it anger, or something more? Thane couldn't be sure, and didn't yet know the questions which might have helped to resolve the point. 'We're checking on several things,' he said, his manner neutral. 'I don't suppose anyone is likely to have seen your boat moored in that cove?' As the other man shook his head, he shrugged. 'Well, we'll see – oh, I'd like a sample of your fingerprints, Preston.

You've been on the Isle at times, and we're trying to eliminate any prints we find.'

'I'll come up to the police station later,' growled Preston. 'Anything else?'

'Not right now, but I'll be back.' Thane gave a brief nod, ignored the other man's glowering stare, and left the wheelhouse. From the deck, he scrambled up on to the quayside and without a backward glance walked in towards the village.

Colin Thane was thoughtful as he entered Inverlay's tiny police office. Almost absent-mindedly he acknowledged the greeting from the constable on duty, walked past him, and entered the station cell where Phil Moss was hard at work using a borrowed typewriter which perched precariously on an old card table. For the moment there was little purpose in spending time trying to analyse Finn Preston's story, or his open and somehow only partly explained dislike of Royan Sonders. Sonders . . . what did they know about him, anyway? He had a yacht, he was supposed to have money – must have, in fact, to run a sea-going luxury craft like the *Gabrielle* and foot the consequent wage bill.

'I said any luck with Preston?' Moss had deserted the typewriter, and was sitting watching him with amusement in his eyes. 'Did you shake hands?'

'And nearly lost mine in the process,' agreed Thane.

'He did the same with me,' groaned Moss. 'Came in looking for you, perfectly civil, how nice to meet you Inspector – and next thing I knew my fingers were being minced. Well, how did it go?'

'According to him, he'd arranged to go to the Isle but chased after shark instead.'

'Believe him?'

'Too early to say.' Thane picked up the telephone, which was stretched to the limit of its lead-wire to reach the cell, and waited for the village switchboard to answer. 'Did you contact Dan Laurence?'

'Yes, and made some progress,' reported his second in command. 'Dan has completed examination of the bottles. No aconite, most of the fingerprints identified as either Tinemann or Willie MacPherson's – Dan took MacPherson's for comparison before he left. That leaves him with only one set unidentified.'

'Which will be Finn Preston's – he's coming here later to give us samples.' Thane broke off as the operator at last answered. He asked for a call to Police Headquarters in Glasgow, then looked up at the cell's single high-set window, three iron bars guarding its space. 'These bars look pretty ancient – wouldn't take much effort to get out of here.'

'Considering the total crime in the last six months has been two poachers, a few assorted drunks and a man who beat up his wife for "private reasons," there's not much cause for worry,' said Moss caustically. 'Oh to be a Highland copper – you're drawing a pension from the day you join.'

At last the call to Glasgow came through and the Headquarters switchboard connected Thane with Buddha Ilford's extension.

Thane made his report, Chief Superintendent Ilford contenting himself with an occasional grunt to indicate he was still listening. When he finished, however, Ilford was ready.

'All right.' The metallic voice was brusque but reasonably friendly. 'I'll see what we can do to check on Sonders – he should be easy enough to trace through the yacht's registration. Well, anything else?'

'Not at the moment,' said Thane cautiously.

'Right.' Buddha Ilford was obviously relieved. 'Never take a desk job, Thane. I'm in the middle of a memorandum for the Chief Constable, subject: clothing allowances for policewomen on plain clothes duty. How the hell do

I know how many pairs of nylons they ladder per month? Huh . . . well, keep in touch.'

The telephone at the other end banged down. Thane replaced his receiver more gently, and was grateful for the sight of two mugs of tea, brought in by the Inverlay constable.

'Thanks.' He took one, sipped approvingly, and then asked, 'Any joy with the coastguard check?'

Phil Moss laid down his tea mug, took the sheet of paper from his typewriter, and handed it over. 'That's all so far – I've a couple more to contact.'

The coastguard stations in the Firth of Lorne area were without exception auxiliary posts, manned by local teams on a bad-weather watch basis. But luckily, the mist on the night Captain Tinemann died had been sufficient to reduce local visibility to near danger limit – which meant most of the posts had been on lookout.

Their reports showed a handful of small cargo coasters on passage through the Firth and the inevitable sprinkling of fishing boats, some unidentified, others noted by their registration numbers. A submarine or a whale – the coast-guard concerned couldn't be positive which – had been carrying out practice dives in deep water. But Moss had underlined two entries logged by the auxiliary stations.

One was from Mull, reporting that a small motor sailer believed to be the *Rock Rose* had been sighted heading for the south-west coast at 9.20 p.m. No other details were available, but it was presumed the vessel was seeking moorings for the night. The second, even briefer, was a note from an Argyll post which said that the *Gabrielle* had been sighted through the mist, heading towards and then past Sanctuary Isle. The time had been minutes after 7 p.m.

Thane took another gulp of tea and rummaged on the card-table until he found the Admiralty chart they'd brought back from the bird warden's hut.

'Give me a hand, Phil . . .' Together, they spread out the rolled-up chart and examined the scattering of islands,

51

large and small. Across from the mainland began the Inner Hebrides, a hydrographic nightmare of rocks and shoals, sea-lochs and tidal drifts. From Inverlay, on the mainland, Thane's finger traced the short sea-distance to Sanctuary Isle then moved on to the massive land-bulk of the island of Mull. To the north lay Lismore, to the south Luing and Scarba, Colonsay and the northern tip of Jura. Around and about each were smaller clusters – uninhabited accidents of nature, mentions in the pilot guides, a nuisance to all but poets and painters.

He studied the chart for a moment, then nodded. 'Well, it fits. Sonders is reported here' – he jabbed – 'going straight past Sanctuary Isle. The yacht moored outside Inverlay harbour about twenty minutes later. That means they didn't have time to double back and approach the Isle from a different direction.'

'But Finn Preston?' Moss let the question hang.

'He's sighted across here.' Thane gestured towards the ragged indentations of Mull's south-west shore. 'The time is as he claims, but there's a devil of a long gap when he's supposed to have been chasing a couple of sharks through the mist.'

'When instead he was maybe landing on Sanctuary Isle?'

'Maybe, Phil. How long till we're due to go out to the Isle?'

'Ten minutes.' At the thought, Moss produced a pillbox from his pocket and slipped one of its contents into his mouth. 'I think I'll go down and make sure MacPherson's ready.'

'I'll wait here.' Thane lifted the telephone as his friend ambled doorwards. 'It's time I phoned home and caught up on my family life.'


It was closer to fifteen minutes later before he made his way to Willie MacPherson's launch. Across the harbour basin the *Rock Rose* was still at her berth, a thin jet of water from her side showing that the Prestons had at last forced their recalcitrant bilge pump into operation.

Inspector Davidson and two other uniformed County police were already aboard the launch, and Phil Moss was standing at the quayside talking to the boatman.

'You're late,' said MacPherson accusingly as he arrived. 'And the tide's on the turn.'

'Sorry.' Thane followed his second in command down the iron ladder set into the quay wall and stepped aboard. Up above, MacPherson cast off the fore and aft lines, then scrambled down while one of the uniformed constables held the launch close to the ladder. The paraffin engine was already ticking over at a noisy rate, and within seconds they were heading out into the Firth. Beyond the harbour's shelter, the launch rolled and shuddered as she met open sea. But it was only a ground swell, and once clear they began making smooth progress, the boat creaking and swaying but moving swiftly under the power of the growling engine.

Thane made his way up beside the boatman, who was at his usual stance by the engine-cover. 'Taking us an easier course today?' he queried innocently.

Just as innocently, MacPherson nodded. 'I'm thinking there's maybe not such a rush, Mr Thane.'

'Good.' Thane raised his voice a little to compete with the engine noise. 'You said the tide was on the turn – does that make it more difficult to get into the Isle?'

The boatman shook his head. 'No, not there. It's The Fangs. The tidal race, Chief Inspector – och, I forgot, you clever folk from the town won't have heard of such things. But it's something any sane man wants to avoid.'

Inspector Davidson had joined them, and the Argyll officer gave a grunt of agreement. 'For once, I'll agree with him, Thane. Remember The Fangs, the half-tide rocks we told you about?'

'Half a mile from the Isle,' Thane nodded.

'Well . . .' Davidson hesitated, then gestured towards the boatman. 'You tell him, MacPherson.'

'Aye, well now.' MacPherson squinted seawards, obviously reducing his explanation to basic terms. 'Imagine the Firth here between Mull and the mainland as a big funnel, Chief Inspector. When the tide is coming in or out then there's an awful lot of water on the move and the entire Atlantic Ocean pushing behind. From the far side of Sanctuary Isle across to Mull it will be normal enough – but there's shoal water from the Isle out to The Fangs, and that means this bit of the funnel isn't working so well. So the water comes galloping and raging through, like a big hairy Highland bull and ten times as dangerous.'

'You mean it affects the current?' Thane had to admit his seamanship was almost non-existent.

'It does that,' said MacPherson with unaccustomed gravity. 'There's a full seven knot race comes shouting down the middle of this channel at its peak – that's when it's halfway to full or ebb tide. And worse between The Fangs and the Isle, with the water being pushed up by the shoal rocks only a fathom or so down. Ten knots it is there, and something to steer well away from. Och, it's safe enough the rest of the time, and we'll be on the Isle before the race begins. But' – he shook his head significantly – 'there's not a man nor beast could be swimming in it when the race is on the move. And I wouldn't even be chancing this boat, even with my mother paying the insurance regular every three months.'

The launch chugged on through the calm, seemingly innocent water while Sanctuary Isle grew larger ahead, its white lighthouse tower gleaming in the warm June sunlight. Two-thirds of the way across, the boatman gave a significant jerk of his head.

On the previous trip across, it had been high tide. Now, at low tide, The Fangs were clearly visible – a jagged ridge of rock perhaps three hundred feet long, up to twenty feet broad at places, the water lapping deceptively against the sharp outcrops, some of the broad crevices between jammed with weed and shingle. Here and there, there was even a smooth patch of rock-imprisoned pebble. The scene tempted a landing, and it would have been easy to reach these pebbled stretches – but it required little imagination to realize why, in different conditions or when the tidal race was on the move, its name was so singularly apt.

'Doesn't look the best place for a picnic,' said Phil Moss cheerfully. The combination of calm seas and blue skies, plus the inner confidence provided by some hefty pre-voyage medication, resulted in him almost enjoying the trip. He loosened his tie and collar and relaxed against the thwarts. It might, he mused, be a good idea to invest in same sun-tan oil. Sunburn could be painful, sometimes even dangerous.

Sanctuary Isle had its usual circling, gliding squadrons of inquiring gulls and other seabirds, some swooping adventurously low to inspect the new arrivals, while others skimmed down to land on the blue-green water, crying loudly in their eternal greedy hope of food. A few seals swam and splashed in the bay, giving an occasional glimpse of the full length of their smooth black bodies as they turned and plunged at play.

The launch slowed, moved gently in towards the flat granite of the landing place, where low tide had exposed fresh weed and shell-covered areas of its bulk, and a few moments later they were ashore. Inspector Davidson and his replacement duty men went off to meet the two constables who had been on overnight guard, carrying with them three large jerricans of fresh water they'd brought from the mainland.

The two Glasgow detectives had other plans. Thane waited patiently until Willie MacPherson had switched off the launch engine and then, as the man scrambled ashore, asked him, 'How about giving us a conducted tour?'

'Why not? It will be doing me no harm to stretch my legs a bit,' agreed the boatman. 'Where would you want to start?'

'At the bonfire beacon – the one Captain Tinemann would light to signal he needed help.'

'That's at the south end,' nodded MacPherson. 'Not far from where I found him lying.'

They followed him over the rocks and into the belt of rustling long grass and thistle-weed beyond, a handful of birds sparking from cover just ahead of them to circle and provide a squawking indignant escort. Beyond the grass they were once more on bare, worn rock, warm to the touch, the sun's glare picking out the glint of thin quartz veins among the grey-black boulders.

They reached the granite ridge, dropped down to the sand and boulder soil beneath, and skirted the spot where the bird warden had died.

'Over here now' – MacPherson turned to the right, heading towards a trio of giant rocks. There, beneath their shelter, was the bonfire beacon a six-foot high pile of driftwood. 'The place was well chosen. There's shelter from the westerly gales, it's fine and dry, and the fire would be attracting anyone looking to sea from Inverlay.'

Phil Moss strolled forward to examine the beacon, pulled at one projecting piece of weathered timber, then frowned and pulled again, heaving the entire length of wood from its place in the middle of the bonfire pile.

'Fine and dry?' he sniffed. 'On the outside, maybe. But not the rest of it.'

Thane and the boatman joined him and saw themselves. The outer foot or so of the wooden spare was bone-dry, but below that the damp began until the portion which had been at the centre of the bonfire was wet to the touch.

'Let's try some more' – Thane began dragging other billets of wood from the beacon pile. His face grew grimmer as he stacked each one to the side. All were the same, dry on the outside, wet where they had formed the heart of the standby alarm. The shingle surface on which the bonfire stood told the same story – the beacon's heart was incapable of bursting into flame.

'Willie . . .' Thane's voice was ominously quiet. 'You said this spot was "fine and dry." I'll take it you meant that the sea couldn't reach it. When was the last time there was rain in this part of the world, a really heavy downpour?'

The boatman bit his lip. 'A good wee while back, Chief Inspector. The weather's been like this, warm and sunny with often a strong wind, for – well, ten days anyway.'

'A strong, drying wind,' growled Phil Moss. 'Which means this bonfire should be ready to go up at the first touch of a match.'

Thane rubbed his chin with one hand, feeling the odd patches of stubble. The Inverlay Arms didn't have electric razor points, and he'd used a borrowed safety razor that morning, with toilet soap as a lather – obviously, he was out of practice.

'There's only one possible reason for this beacon being wet. Someone damped it down with water, damped it down thoroughly enough to make quite sure it couldn't be used. The bird warden had to die, and he wasn't to be given the chance of raising an alarm.'

Willie MacPherson gave a faint shudder. 'So maybe Captain Tinemann did reach here after all,' he murmured. 'And if the poor soul couldn't be getting the wood to burn –'

'He'd lost his last chance of life.' Thane put it bluntly. 'There's an easy enough way to prove it. Tinemann had a cigarette lighter in his pocket, and no matches. Let's see if he tried to use paper to set the fire going.'

Inch by inch they searched round the base of the wood-pile, gradually widening their circle. Phil Moss was first to find the tragic links they needed, fragments of blackened paper and paper ash which had been blown by the wind into a crevice at the foot of one of the three giant rocks.

'Willie, how positive are you that no one else knew Captain Tinemann had run out of liquor?' Thane put it almost casually, apparently giving most of his attention to watching Moss gather each minute portion of their latest evidence. One by one the thin wiry figure slid paper fragments on to sheets torn from his notebook, pressed

57

another sheet on top of each, then put the whole collection into the inevitable transparent plastic envelope.

'Willie?'

The boatman took a half-hearted kick at a smooth round pebble. 'I told you, nobody else knew,' he said gruffly.

Willie MacPherson was uneasy, almost certainly lying. But for the moment . . . Thane gave a faint shrug. 'All right,' he nodded. 'Let's get on with it.'

In the distance, the Isle's half-mile length was deceptive. At some parts the going was easy. But at others they had to scramble over slippery green-slimed rock, skirt deep pools and inlets, test each uncertain foothold. Two-thirds of the way along the north shore, at a point just beyond the lighthouse tower, the boatman halted.

'There's an old well near here, Chief Inspector,' said MacPherson, pointing towards a patch of bright green rush-grass which was overlooked by a ridge of granite rock. 'Mr Hollis was telling me once that the Bird Society meant to clean it out and see if it could be used again.' As they followed him over to a point a little below the ridge, he explained, 'Nowadays, all the fresh water has to brought out from the mainland. There's a big twenty-gallon tank behind the warden's hut, and I had to bring out enough to fill it each supply trip.'

Some work appeared to have already been done on the well project. Its lip, an edging of boulders jammed tight together, showed signs of recent repair. For a few feet down, the shaft itself had been cleared, and an accumulation of stone, sand and other clogging debris had been piled to one side. But the task was still far from complete – looking into the well, Thane saw a solid, close-packed mass of stone and shingle, still waiting to be removed.

He straightened up again and looked around. Not far away, there was the rough outline of what, at some distant time, must have been the foundation walls of a small stone cottage.

'Willie, how long since the well was in use or anyone really lived here?'

'Maybe hundreds of years, Chief Inspector. I doubt if anyone knows, not even my old mother – and her so full of the tales of these parts that the radio people came up from London to talk to her.'

'For a folklore programme?'

'Aye, that's what they called it,' agreed MacPherson. 'It was a regular invasion, a collection of thin wee men wi' tape recorders and wonderful expense accounts. Every time my mother would stop they were at her to remember something else . . . and paying her money for every story.'

'A good aid to memory,' said Thane with a slow grin.

'Or the imagination,' twinkled the boatman. 'Och well, the souls were happy at the end of it, and my old mother is the great one with the stories. Well now, shall we be moving on? I can take you right up to the rocks at the north end, where the seals make their home. After that, we can be heading back towards the warden's hut.'

'Lead on,' nodded Thane.

# Chapter Three

The bird warden's hut was a more cheerful place, thanks to the efforts of the two guard-duty constables who had used it as their overnight headquarters. A driftwood fire was burning in the open hearth, there was a slightly stale but still welcoming smell of pipe tobacco, and a small pile of breakfast dishes, washed and left to dry, were lying to one side of the little washtub.

Willie MacPherson had gone back to wait by his boat. The guard-duty men and their reliefs, idle for the moment, were gossiping together a few yards from the hut doorway and keeping one eye on Inspector Davidson as the county officer made a prowling tour of the area.

Inside the hut, Colin Thane was also on the prowl – but with more definite purpose. He moved from wall to wall, examining cupboards, tapping, probing. By his side, Phil Moss carried out the same routine with slightly less fervour.

'It would help if we knew what we were looking for,' he grumbled.

'Call it a needle in a haystack if you have to have a label,' said Thane. For the second time he emptied the food cupboard, checked its contents, and returned them one by one to their shelves. Gloomily, Moss continued his own task until Thane at last called a halt.

'Store shed next.'

As the two detectives left the hut, the constabulary quartet broke off their conversation, then, seeing both men head round to the rear of the hut, relaxed again. Aye, the

60

C.I.D. were busy – but, after all, that was what they were paid for, and there were times when volunteers simply got in the road.

The store shed was little more than an outside extension of the warden's hut, its plain wooden door shut by a simple bolt and socket. Thane slid the bolt, and the door creaked back on salt-air rusted hinges. Within, there was just enough standing room for one man, the rest of the space piled high with a miscellaneous collection of Crusoe-type hardware ranging from a pick and shovel to a thick coil of manilla rope.

'We'll empty it,' he decided. 'I'll hand the things out.'

Buckets, paint cans, more rope, two spare cylinders of bottled gas – the pile grew rapidly. The Scottish Sea Bird Society couldn't be accused of failing to cater for most eventualities. As the pile thinned, the metal shape of the water tank became clearly visible.

'Here's something.' Thane stretched out an arm, managed to get his fingers to the edge of a piece of coarse sacking, and gave it a jerk. The sacking, wrapped round a long, fairly heavy object, moved a little but there was more resistance than he'd expected. He cleared more space, and tried again. This time it slid clear, and Phil Moss squeezed in beside him to help unwrap the bundle.

'Ach, it's just a piece of old wood.' Moss's voice was a mixture of puzzlement and disappointment.

'But very old and pretty heavy,' said Thane as they examined their find. 'Oak, I think.' The wood, stave-shaped, had a ragged break at one end and was dented and splintered at several places along its length.

'What's it doing in here?' Moss ran a finger along its surface, and stopped short as a splinter jabbed into his flesh.

'He probably found it on the beach,' shrugged Thane. 'It's from some ship or boat, that's certain – Tinemann would have an eye open for any flotsam like this as raw material for his wood-carving.' He put the wood down, and foraged in the few remaining corners of the shed.

61

'Inside the water tank?' His companion named the last remaining possibility.

The tank's main inlet was outside the shed, but there was also a hatch on its top surface, for cleaning or inspection. Phil Moss took off his jacket, rolled up his shirt sleeve, and plunged his arm in almost to the shoulder. He groped blindly for a moment, then shook his head. 'Nothing – except some dam' cold water.'

Two of the otherwise unemployed county men outside were detailed to load the stores back into the shed. Their companions grinned, then switched off their smiles as Thane went past.

'The big fellow doesn't look over happy,' muttered one of them, refastening his tunic top button. The other nodded, and decided against refilling his pipe.

It was another hour before the tide's state was right to allow them to leave the Isle. Only when Willie MacPherson was satisfied that the race of water over the shoal rock leading out to The Fangs had died sufficiently would he agree to cast off and head back to the mainland.

In the stern of the launch, Thane sat beside Inspector Davidson, watching the two Argyll constables they'd left on guard begin the toiling scramble from the landing place back to the hut.

'Willie' – he waited until the boatman had turned from his post by the ancient engine, 'if Royan Sonders' yacht is still at her moorings I want to go aboard. Okay?' Willie MacPherson gave a wave of acknowledgement, and Thane nodded briefly to his second-in-command. 'Better come along too, Phil. At the least, we'll have a free tour over the boat.'

Sonders' deep-draught forty tonner was, as he'd hoped, still bow-moored in the deep water a little way outside Inverlay harbour. A crewman was dangling over the *Gabrielle's* port side in a bo'sun's chair, paintbrush in hand as he touched up some minor flaw in the hull's powder blue finish. Another seaman, dressed in jeans and singlet, leaned casually against the white superstructure and watched the launch approach. As it came alongside, he slouched over to the lowered companionway ladder, tossed his cigarette stub into the water, and waited unconcernedly while the two detectives stepped from the launch, grabbed the ladder's side-rope in turn, and climbed on deck beside him.

'Mr Sonders aboard?' queried Thane.

The man nodded and promptly walked away . . . Thane remembered him as being almost equally uncommunicative when they had had their shore-based interview session with the *Gabrielle's* crew. While they waited, he gave a quick wave of his hand to the launch below. Its engine quickened as it headed away from the *Gabrielle*, steering towards the harbour.

The seaman returned in a couple of minutes, Royan Sonders by his side. The paunchy yacht owner's gold tooth flashed as he gave a beam of welcome.

'Chief Inspector Thane – and Inspector Moss! Welcome aboard.' He turned to the deck hand. 'Peroz, tell Gino to bring some coffee to my day-cabin.' As the man went off on his errand, Sonders beamed again. 'I saw the launch heading out towards Sanctuary Isle this morning, and wondered if you'd stop here on your way back to shore. Well, how do you like my *Gabrielle*?'

The yacht had been impressive enough from a distance. Now, aboard her, surrounded by sparkling paint and gleaming metal-work, the impression of clean strength of line, of functional beauty of design, was still further enhanced. The South African kept his craft in precise style – even the big motor launch slung on davits by her stern reflected the same glistening readiness. By comparison, the *Gabrielle's* crew of four seemed sloppy in their turnout – but that was Sonders' affair.

'She looks nice to me,' Thane told the *Gabrielle's* owner, and Phil Moss muttered similar sentiments.

'I don't mind admitting I'm pretty proud of her,' declared Sonders. 'Come on, I'll show you some more.' He shepherded them ahead of him.

63

Sixty feet long, the *Gabrielle* had obviously been built with no economy restrictions on her fittings. Two large staterooms lay aft, bright and airy, separated by a thick soundproof bulk-head from the engine-room with its gleaming twin 50 h.p. diesels. As they passed through the control area, they had to squeeze past another of the French crewmen, busy with oilcan and cleaning rag. He gave them only a brief glance before continuing his task.

'What sort of speed can she give you?' asked Thane, glancing round the complicated layout of fuel pipes, control rods and gauges.

'Twelve, maybe fourteen knots. I am more concerned with reliability.' Sonders led them up on deck again, up another short iron-railed ladder, and into the wheelhouse bridge, big and roomy compared with the box-like structure Thane had seen aboard Finn Preston's *Rock Rose*. Radar, echo-sounding, short-wave radio, duplicate control panels and constant-view vision ports were only a few of its features. There was even a series of central heating radiators mounted round its length. 'Aft, I've got what I call my day-cabin. Below deck, the main saloon – the crew quarters are up for'ard.'

A faint buzz came from the intercom phone by his side. He lifted the receiver, listened, gave a grunt, and then replaced it.

'Later, we can take in the rest. But for now' – he slapped his paunch, a drum-like blow – 'coffee is waiting.'

They followed him out of the wheelhouse and down to the day-cabin, a small thick-glassed deckhouse, neatly fitted with couch, table, chairs and a roll-top desk. A plain-finished brass tray with coffee jugs and the necessary china was lying on the table.

Sonders busied himself pouring. 'I take black. Chief Inspector –?'

'Black for me,' agreed Thane.

'Very white,' requested Phil Moss, his ulcer in mind.

The South African handed round the cups. 'Right, Chief

Inspector. Let's get down to business – I don't imagine this is your time for social calls.'

Thane sipped his coffee, settled back on the couch, and gave a faint frown. 'I'll be diplomatic and call it both. You told me you saw Finn Preston's boat heading towards the Isle, and as far as timing is concerned we've had outside confirmation. But Preston says you must also have seen him veer off course, chasing after a couple of sharks – he says he cut across your bows.'

Royan Sonders gave a snort. 'I'd have remembered it if he did. Sorry, Chief Inspector, I saw him on course, then I lost him in the mist. That's all I know.'

'You don't particularly like one another, do you?'

'He hates my guts, and I think he is . . . well, I return the sentiment. But that does not matter at this time. I have told you what I saw.'

'Two of your crew confirm your story, the other two were below deck,' said Phil Moss. 'We had a bit of a job with one of them – he had darned little English, and my French is almost zero.'

'That would be Jehan.' Sonders gave a grunt of amusement. 'Sometimes it can be difficult, but they work well. The *Gabrielle* is French registered, of course, and I inherited the crew when I bought her over.'

'There's another point I want to clear up.' Thane put down the coffee cup. 'We checked through the bird sanctuary visitors book, and your name is in it once only. But it seems Captain Tinemann didn't always log his guests. Were you out at any other time?'

'Twice more.' Sonders answered easily, walked across to the roll-top desk and opened it. 'Here's the reason.' He showed them a small, beautifully carved wooden figure of a seabird, its wings spread ready for flight. 'Captain Tinemann made it – I saw it half-completed the first time I was out, decided I wanted it, and went back to see him. We did a deal, and I took a trip out in the speedboat about a couple of days later to collect it. I gave him a carton of cigarettes, and we were both happy.'

'Thanks, Mr Sonders.' Thane got up. 'Now, the only problem remaining is, how do we get ashore?'

'Peroz will take you in on the runabout,' said the yacht owner. 'She's tied up alongside.'

They went out on deck, and Sonders gave a bellow. As Peroz appeared, the South African began to give him the order then stopped with an angry growl. Her engine beating a smooth, regular pulse, the *Rock Rose* had cleared the Inverlay harbour entrance and was sailing towards them, a white wake boiling from her stern as the propellor responded to full throttle.

'Preston. This is his idea of a joke every time he comes out.' Royan Sonders didn't try to disguise the anger in his voice as the broad-beamed motor sailer came closer. 'A beat-up, I think they call it.'

Finn Preston was at the wheel, and the boat was close enough now to see the finest detail of her deck gear. As she swept past, only inches from the *Gabrielle's* side, Preston stuck his head through the opened wheel-house window and gave a roar of laughter. 'Hello there! You're in poor company, Chief Inspector!'

Sonders gripped the deck-rail, knuckles white, but said nothing. The *Rock Rose* held her course right down the length of the luxury yacht, an arms-length short of collision, then headed on arrow-straight out into the Firth.

'Next time he tries that, I'll turn a deck-hose on his lousy butcher-boat,' growled Sonders. 'The man's a maniac.'

The 'runabout', the white-hulled speedboat Thane had seen at the Isle the previous day, was tied up by the *Gabrielle's* stern. The deckhand brought it round to the companionway ladder where it waited, engines throbbing.

'Hey, I almost forgot,' declared Sonders. 'Will the police object if I leave the yacht for a couple of days?' The South African tucked his thumbs into his broad leather belt. 'The day after tomorrow I'm supposed to fly to Switzerland – I've got business in Lucerne. With luck, I'll be back the following day.'

'If it's important, go ahead,' Thane told him. 'But

66

remember that you're a witness in this case – I'd like to know the moment you get back.'

Sonders promised, and the two detectives clambered down to the speedboat. Once they were aboard, its twin outboard motors spat to full life. The lightweight craft bucked away from the *Gabrielle* in a cloud of spray, a short hectic journey which ended as the seaman throttled back just inside the harbour entrance. The speedboat's bow lowered, and it glided in to nudge to a halt beside a flight of worn stone steps in the quayside wall. Peroz acknowledged their thanks with a truculent nod. As soon as they had started on their way up the stairway he had the speedboat growling on its return trip.

Side by side, the two detectives walked along the quay towards the village. The harbour was quiet, the fishing boats out on the start of their long workday, a handful of small craft the only remaining vessels moored in the basin, two grizzled old men repairing the vast expanse of a herring net the only sign of work in progress.

'Oh – oh! I wondered when they'd arrive.' Thane gave a growl as he saw the familiar little group gathered at the harbour gate. The newsmen were about a dozen strong, including a trio of duffel-coated photographers.

'Better late than never, Mr Thane,' greeted their red-headed leader, Jock Mills of the *Bugle*. 'How's Inspector Moss bearing up? Been sea-sick yet?'

'If I ever am, Jock, I can think of a good use for that rag you call a newspaper,' sniffed the indignant victim of his wit. 'What kept you so long?'

'We didn't know a thing about it until this morning,' said the reporter. 'Then somebody called MacPherson, the local boatman, got busy. He seems to have phoned every paper in the business.'

'And made himself a nice little bag of gold,' grunted one of his colleagues. 'We wired him five quid for the tip-off.'

'Our news desk sent him ten,' chimed a second.

'I might have guessed.' Colin Thane decided to notch

Willie MacPherson's business acumen another couple of points up his scale.

'That's only the beginning,' complained Jock Mills. 'He's sitting in the hotel bar now, offering a signed account of how he found the body – on sale to the highest bidder.'

'They're simple people, these Highlanders,' said Phil Moss unsympathetically. 'If you're polite, he'll maybe give you it on hire-purchase.'

'Your ulcer's showing,' poked Jock Mills. 'Well, Mr Thane, what's the score? Can we quote you that it is murder?'

Thane was silent for a moment, then he shrugged. 'All right, you know the bones of the situation. The bird warden on Sanctuary Isle was found dead. Inspector Moss and I have been sent to work with the Argyll police, and it has been established that the warden – Captain Tinemann – died from aconite poisoning. If you want to know what that is, look up an encyclopædia. Tinemann had one known relative, an elderly woman, and I'm not telling you where she lives.'

'And it was murder?' Two reporters asked the question almost simultaneously.

'How about "foul play is suspected"?'

They groaned, and he relented. 'All right, it was murder. That's all I can give you.'

With a murmur of thanks the pressmen began to drift away, the evening paper reporters to telephone a quick add to their earlier stories, the morning men to digest the situation and then decide whether or not to haggle with the hard-headed business man waiting in the bar of the Inverlay Arms.

At the police station, another visitor waited them. Edgar Hollis rose from his seat as they entered and cleared his throat in nervous style. 'I – ah – hope you don't mind my lying in wait for you like this' – the little man hesitated.

'Any time,' acknowledged Thane. 'What can we do for you, Mr Hollis?'

'It's about the Isle and the publicity that's starting – I've already had two reporters attempting to interview me.'

'And there will be more,' said Moss.

'I don't mind that – what I mean is, I don't like it, but it isn't the most important factor.' Hollis blinked, swallowed, and went on. 'I want to know what's going to happen on the Isle. We're in the nesting season, and with poor Tinemann dead, my committee may decide to appoint another warden.'

'Well, we'll have a police guard out there for a few days yet,' Thane reassured him. 'Nobody will be allowed to land without permission. After that, it's up to you.'

'Good. Thank you, Chief Inspector.' The news seemed to lift a considerable weight from the Scottish Sea Bird Society official.

'How's your back behaving today?' asked Moss. 'The pain any better?'

'Not too bad, not too bad,' said Hollis. 'Well, I must be on my way now.'

'Going home to Oban?' Thane picked up the small bundle of report sheets lying on the station officer's desk and glanced at their headings.

'No, not for some time. I have one or two clients in the area, and I may as well look them up while I'm here.' Hollis backed towards the door, gave an almost comical bow, and left them.

Only two of the report sheets belonged to the Tinemann case. The first, a telephone message from Dan Laurence in Glasgow, was a categorical statement that the sample set of fingerprints received earlier that day matched the only previously unidentified samples on the liquor bottles taken from Tinemann's hut.

The second, longer and typewritten, had been prepared by the station sergeant. It reported that Finn Preston had called as arranged, had volunteered fingerprint samples, and that these had been despatched – news outdated by the telephone message. The rest of its length boiled down to the fact that the round-up check of doctors and chemists in a wide area of the county had drawn a blank. There was no recent prescription or purchase of aconite, no known industrial use for the poison in the area.

'What's the time?'

Phil Moss glanced at his watch. 'Leaving 3 p.m. Why?'

'I haven't eaten since breakfast, that's why,' complained Thane. 'Let's get down to the hotel and see if we can organize a sandwich. After that, we're going to split up and start knocking on doors. I want to tune into the village gossip grapevine – two questions, Phil. Did Willie MacPherson even hint to anyone that Tinemann had run out of liquor? Did anyone who saw the *Gabrielle* tie up at her moorings that evening make an accurate count of how many men were aboard?'

His companion gave a soft whistle. 'Just in case someone dropped off in that little speedboat and went for a journey! I'm with you.' He pulled the plastic envelope from his pocket and laid it on the desk. 'What about these bits of burnt paper?'

'Leave them for the moment,' Thane told him. 'Unless we come up with a spectacular piece of evidence – and we won't – I'm driving back to the city in the morning. You stay and hold the fort, Phil – I'll be back. There are a few items I want to have a closer look at, and I can't do it up here. I'll hand these fragments in to the Scientific Bureau as soon as I reach Glasgow, and let you know the moment there's any result through.'

A sandwich and then a door-knocking session; Phil Moss grimaced, patted one pocket to make sure his pill supply was in its place, and for the hundredth time decided to apply for the next Headquarters nine-till-five desk job that fell vacant.


It went pretty much as Thane had prophesied. Several hours of door-knocking interviews, during which the two C.I.D. men refused gallons of tea and at least a pint of the stronger stuff, ended with almost the entire village population having been canvassed. The questions took time, had to be planted with care as seemingly casual requests in the middle of apparently weightier but utterly useless conversation. The net results were nil.

Wakened at six the next morning, Thane washed, shaved, dressed and remained in a sleepy-eyed daze throughout most of the car journey to Glasgow. The police driver, a county man, made an estimated half-dozen remarks about the weather and spent the rest of the time sucking peppermints.

The car reached the city a little before 9 a.m., edged its way along the busy length of Clyde Street, turned left past the sombre bulk of the High Court building and the squat red-brick outline of its companion, the city mortuary, and a few moments later drew into the garage yard at Headquarters.

Thane made his first call the Scientific Bureau. Superintendent Laurence hadn't yet arrived, but the young detective constable at the duty desk promised to hand Laurence the paper-ash fragments as soon as he showed up.

Next stop was Buddha Ilford's office. As city C.I.D. boss, Chief Superintendent Ilford made a point of being in early, whatever the season. Thane pressed the buzzer button outside the dark-shadowed doorway, waited in the corridor until the signal indicator beside it lit up the 'enter' label, then went in.

Buddha Ilford, his favourite pipe billowing blue smoke, his newspaper opened at the comic-strip section, raised one bushy eyebrow in slight surprise, sucked his pipe again, and demanded, 'What the devil are you doing here?' He gestured towards the chair opposite and, as Thane sat down, closed the paper.

'I brought down some stuff I wanted the Scientific Bureau to have a look at. And the telephone isn't the best way of checking on some other items I've got in mind.'

'Mmmph.' Buddha accepted the explanation. 'Well, hav-

71

ing you here saves me a phone call of my own. Wait a minute' – he rummaged through the small mountain of overnight reports in his desk tray – 'here we are. A run-down on your yacht-owning pal Royan Sonders. Interpol had to be dragged in to help put it together. Royan Sonders, age 43, mixed British-Boer extraction, left South Africa about five years ago, no police record there. Now has financial interests in Switzerland, legitimate, though maybe on thin ice occasionally. Ach, you know the sort of thing. Sell something you haven't got to Mr A, then buy it with money you haven't got from Mr B and end up with a profit. All the best middlemen do it.'

'And the wealthy yachtsman part, sir?'

'I'm coming to that.' Buddha Ilford gave a growl, puffed slowly and deliberately on his pipe, and paraphrased the next portion of the Interpol report. 'The *Gabrielle* is regis-tered in his name all right. He bought it in Calais in early March, after it had been laid up for a spell. Sonders has a yacht master's ticket – South African issued. The yacht was paid for by a draft drawn on a Swiss bank, and you know what that means. It practically takes a Government order before a Swiss banker will volunteer what year it is. But the Swiss police can tell us this – Sonders bases himself on Lucerne, and hasn't been doing any business since the beginning of the year. He spread the word he'd pulled off a big-money deal and was going to have himself a holiday. In other words, Colin, you're up a gum tree unless you've something else to go on. Why'd he want to kill the bird warden anyway?'

Thane felt a surge of disappointment. 'I don't know,' he admitted. 'In fact, I don't know why anybody would. If Tinemann had had his head bashed in, I'd probably ignore Sonders and have Finn Preston in a cell by now. But Preston doesn't seem the poisoning type.'

'Neither does the canteen cook, but she does her best,' grunted Ilford. 'You're stranded. Admit it.'

'No sir.' Thane refused to accept the C.I.D. chief's ver-dict. 'I didn't come down to dump the case back in your lap. This report. . . . Interpol say the yacht had been laid up, don't they?'

Buddha Ilford gave a nod.

'But Sonders told me he inherited her crew when he took it over from the previous owner.'

'The four Frenchmen.' The Chief Superintendent sat silent for a moment or two, puffing his pipe, his face in the state of rotund contemplation which had earned him his irreverent nickname. 'All right, we'll send names and descriptions to Interpol and see what they say about 'em. What else have you got?'

Thane told him the rest of the story to date. Ilford showed a faint stirring of interest once or twice, but made no comment until he'd finished.

'Preston seems a wild enough character,' he grimaced. 'How about his wife's story? Was she visiting friends?'

'That's definite,' said Thane. 'The county police checked it through.'

'Just a thought,' murmured the Chief Superintendent. 'Incidentally, I'll tell Interpol that Sonders is making this visit to Switzerland . . . they can keep a casual eye on him for us.' He glanced at his watch. 'All right, Colin, leave it at that. There's a High Court sitting today, and I'll need to get over to it soon.'

Thane took the hint. As he left, Buddha Ilford opened his paper again and returned to the strip section. With a day at the High Court ahead, a man needed some light relief.

It was almost noon before the Scientific Bureau managed to complete the task he'd given them, but Thane put in the time without any difficulty – there were a couple of Millside Division cases which also strayed within the province of the Fraud Squad, and he seized the chance to sort out the situation.

When he finally entered the Scientific Bureau office, Superintendent Laurence looked up and gave a growl. 'Practically breathing down our necks for this, aren't you?' he complained. 'It's ready, but only just.'

'Sorry, Dan. Business is brisk.'

'Forget it,' grumped the white-haired Bureau chief. He brushed an accumulation of cigarette ash from his crumpled waistcoat and nodded towards the nearest lab table. 'Come and see if you can make any sense out of this lot.'

The Bureau team had done their best with the fragments of burnt paper and ash Thane had brought them. Moistened with an atomizer spray of shellac and alcohol, pressed between glass plates in as near complete state as possible, the fragments had then been photographed in an ultra-violet light.

'I'd have liked it better if we could have collected the bits ourselves,' rumbled Dan Laurence. 'It's delicate work, Colin. Some of the ash had crumbled to dust when we got it.'

'If we'd waited, the wind would probably have blown the lot half across the Isle.' Thane puzzled over the photographs, the fragments showing as ragged-edged black or grey, some pieces blank, others with recaptured writing etched in white over their surface.

'I've been having a wee try at it myself,' said the Bureau chief. 'It looks to me as if he burned two separate pieces of paper, each maybe quarto size. One seems to have been a list of birds. See here' – he pointed to one of the prints – 'it's laid out like some sort of points table. Common gull, herring gull, lesser black backed, greater black backed, Arctic tern. . . . I can't make out the next one.'

'Probably a check list he carried,' agreed Thane. 'One of his jobs was to keep tabs on the types of bird as they arrived. What's this other one?'

'Damned if I know.' Dan Laurence rubbed his upper lip. 'It looks like a part of an arithmetic problem. But don't jump to any wild conclusions, Colin. It's neither a scientific formula nor an exercise in navigation – I've tried that angle.'

Thane peered down at the figures. 'One thousand five fifty-six, one five eighty-eight,' he glanced at Laurence and was rewarded with a faint shake of the head. 'Then this bit here, different figures in combined multiplication and division – all right, Dan, I give up.'

'You're not alone,' sighed Laurence ruefully. 'Old MacMaster looked in earlier, and I tried it out on him. He hadn't a clue either – so if a university professor can't get it, why should two ignorant coppers worry?'

'MacMaster?' Thane was interested. 'When did he get back?'

'Last night. Said he found it a most interesting post mortem.' Dan Laurence wrinkled his nose and gave a fair imitation of the forensic expert's precise tones. '"A refreshing change from the usual run of the mill, Superintendent – a poisoning and an unusual one at that." You'll need to arrest someone, Colin. MacMaster's just dying to get into the witness box and be let loose.'

'I'll try and oblige.' Thane took out his cigarettes, handed one to Dan Laurence, and struck a match.

'Thanks.' Laurence took a long drag on the cigarette then blew a smoke cloud skywards. 'What now? Heading back to Inverlay?'

Thane shook his head. 'Not for a while yet, I've got enough on my plate to keep me going until late afternoon. Then, if I can manage, I'll nip home for a meal before going north.'

'Well, the best of luck,' growled Laurence. 'It looks as though you're going to need it.'

Thane had a quick sandwich and coffee in the Headquarters canteen, then set out on his programme. First on the list was the local office of the shipping line which had formerly employed Captain Tinemann. The branch manager dug deep into the line's files, and confirmed that Tinemann had been aboard a ship torpedoed in World War II – and that a young cadet F. Preston had been among the survivors.

The same branch manager had plenty of contacts in most branches of the world of shipping and the sea. Half an hour later, Thane was in another quiet office in an even duller looking building. The man at the other side of the old-fashioned desk was thin, prematurely grey, and agreed that his firm were in the shark liver business.

'We rend them down for oil, of course,' he explained. 'The whole thing is a strictly commercial operation . . . shark oil is in a class all its own for some technical processes.'

'So Preston is on a good thing financially?'

The other man smiled sourly. 'He was. The market isn't as good as it used to be, and where he might have earned £100 a fish a year ago he's probably lucky if he gets a quarter of that now. It's dangerous work, Chief Inspector. A basking shark can't bite, but one whack from its tail can smash a fair-sized boat to matchwood – not to mention a nasty habit it has of surfacing under a boat's keel. Any money Preston gets, he earns.'

'Prices have fallen,' mused Thane. 'How does that leave him?'

'Presuming you've got a good reason for asking, tight for money. We helped him pay the last fuel bill for the *Rock Rose*, though I believe he's gathering a little more cash now, shooting seals as a sideline.'

Thane thanked him, and went on to his next interview session. The chairman of the Scottish Sea Bird Society, a retired colonel, took a little time to thaw out on the subject of Edgar Hollis. When he did, his comments amounted to a stout stonewall defence of a little Oban chartered accountant.

'Some people think we're cranks, Thane . . . damn fools more concerned with birds than humans. But someone's got to do it – the world's wildlife is being exterminated. That goes for both birds and animals. It's calculated that in ten years the only survivors among some breeds will be specimens behind bars in a zoo. That's why there's a World Wildlife Fund – and if their trustees are cranks, then I'm in damn good company. Sanctuary Isle and places like it are saving birds from extinction at the hands of unthinking idiots.'

76

'And Mr Hollis?' Thane steered him back.

'I've told you before. Hollis is, to use that old-fashioned phrase, a good man. Plays around with guns a bit, but wouldn't harm a fly. Well' – he frowned – 'I saw him go bald-headed at a fellow once. Hollis caught him smashing birds' eggs against a wall. I had to drag Hollis off the man before he . . .'

'Before he killed the fellow?'

The Bird Society chairman shifted uncomfortably. 'I wasn't going to use those words. And there was provocation.'

'There often is,' agreed Thane. 'Well, that's all for just now, sir.'

He finally reached home a little before 5 p.m. The small suburban bungalow was identical with a hundred others in the same street – except, he had to admit, that the front garden grass required cutting more than most lawns around and the rose bushes were in urgent need of an anti-blight spray. Gardening was the privilege of civil servants, bookmakers and other characters who could plan their life with routine purpose.

'Colin!' Mary Thane opened the door as he was about to put his key in the lock. 'What are you doing here?'

'Everyone seems to be asking me that today,' he complained. 'I thought the place might fall down if I stayed away too long.' He gave her an affectionate peck on the lips, then the living room door opened in the background and a leggy avalanche of Boxer dog and children descended on them. Digging into his pockets for the fishing line and shell necklace presents he'd brought the youngsters from Inverlay, giving the excited pup its expected quota of rib-thumping pats, Thane surrendered to his family role.

By the time their evening meal was finished, the pup was asleep on his back by the fireside, Tommy and Kate were arguing over whose turn it was to help with the washing-up, and Sanctuary Isle seemed distant.

77

He sighed. 'I'd like to stay, Mary. But Phil's expecting me back tonight.'

'Any more progress?' She poured him a second cup of tea.

'It gets more complicated every step we take,' he admitted. 'I thought we might be on to something when Dan Laurence's boys managed to decipher some notes Tinemann had had to burn. But all we're left with is what looks like one of Tommy's arithmetic problems. Unrelated figures mostly – I can't make sense out of 'em.'

'Sounds like Tommy's arithmetic too,' said his wife wryly. 'I had to spend an hour sorting out his homework last night.' There was humour in her voice, yet she felt concern. In all their marriage she'd come to accept that when her husband talked about a case it meant he was far from happy about the way it was shaping.

'One thousand five fifty-six, one five eighty-eight.' Thane grimaced. 'It must mean something I suppose.'

'Dad' – his son, alerted by the mention of his name, broke off the dish-washing argument.

'Not just now, Tommy.' Mary Thane frowned across the table.

'But –'

The boy's second attempt was interrupted by the sudden clamour of the telephone bell.

'I'm expecting a call – I'll get it.' Thane rose from his place, crossed over, and lifted the receiver. 'Hello – Thane here.'

'Ah, at last!' Professor MacMaster's thin precise tones came over the wire. 'I thought I might – ah – pass on a little item of advice, Thane. Outwith my sphere in a way, but still –'

'Advice is always welcome.' The burly detective winked in his wife's direction.

'I wondered if you'd come across anyone suffering from neuralgia in the course of – ah – your inquiries.'

'What?' The forensic expert's words took a moment to sink in.

'Neuralgia – nerve pains in the body.' MacMaster gave an impatient cluck. 'One method of treatment is the external application of a special liniment which has aconite as its active ingredient. Highly diluted, of course. But it could still be lethal.'

'Thanks, professor.' A little, tweed-clad man wincing as he scrambled ashore from an open boat. 'It helps – maybe a lot.'

He pressed down the receiver rest, let it free again, and dialled the trunk exchange. Again luck seemed to be running his way, and the call to Inverlay police station got through to that tiny unit to catch Phil Moss just as that long-suffering individual had been about to go out.

'Interesting, very interesting,' agreed his second-in-command. 'So if Edgar Hollis has been using aconite liniment . . .'

'Then our Bird Society convenor has some explaining ahead,' growled Thane. 'Phil, I'm coming straight up by car. Hollis lives in Oban. I want to locate his doctor, find out if any such prescription has been issued to him, and then go on to Hollis's home. If he's awkward, lay on a search warrant. I'll meet you there.'

'Right.' Phil's voice was crisp. The urgency was infectious.

Thane replaced the phone. 'Mary, I'll use our own car to get in to Millside. Phone them for me, and tell them I want the duty car ready and waiting – it'll save some time.'

'But Dad' – his son tried again.

'Sorry, Tommy, I'm in a rush.' On his way to the door, he glanced at his watch. Six-fifteen. With luck and a fast driver, he could reach Oban by eight-forty at the latest.

It didn't work quite as he'd planned. The police Jaguar was snarling its way along the long straight of the A816 road north of Kilmartin, carving its way through the quiet traffic of early evening, when the uniformed driver gave a mutter of annoyance and took his foot off the accelerator pedal. A little way on ahead, a black patrol car was parked at an angle by the roadside while one of its crew flapped his arm in an agitated flagging-down signal.

As the Jaguar halted beside the patrol car, Thane wound down his window and stuck his head out. 'What's up?'

'We've been waiting for you, sir,' said the patrol man. 'Couldn't contact you by radio – your car's on a different frequency from the county units. Inspector Moss wants you to divert to Inverlay police station – he's heading back there from Oban. He said to tell you that Edgar Hollis is missing from home.'

As the Jaguar snarled off on its new course, the patrol man was joined by his mate. 'Well? What did he say?'

The patrol man shook his head. 'I couldn't be repeating it, Lachie, for it would lose in the telling. But it was powerful strong, powerful strong!'

# Chapter Four

The soft sunlight of Highland mid-evening charmed warm pastel colour and shade to life in the broad panorama of sea and hills which came into view as the car topped the last rise before the downhill descent to Inverlay. White smoke curled from the chimneys of the company of little grey-roofed houses which formed a root-bulb to the wide arms of the harbour breakwater. Nearer, a cluster of shaggy broadhorned Highland cattle snorted and stared as the Jaguar went past, dirt and gravel spurting from under its tyres as it cornered on the dusty, winding road.

Chief Detective Inspector Colin Thane was in no mood for scenic soliloquies. He lit another cigarette, drew on it impatiently, then, as the car entered the village main street, ground the long stub's tip on the dashboard ashtray. He swung the car's door open as the Jaguar drew to a halt outside the police station, and was on his way before his driver had cut the engine.

Inside the building, a uniformed constable snapped to attention.

'Inspector Moss?'

'At the hotel, sir. And' – the constable gaped as Thane turned on his heel and stormed out again.

The two men met in the street midway between the police office and the Inverlay Arms.

'I saw your car arrive,' said Moss. 'You made good time.'

'With reason,' barked Thane. 'What's the picture?'

'Hollis hasn't been home since yesterday morning, when

81

he came over to Inverlay – remember, he looked in on us. He seems to have spent most of the time here, and one of the last times he was seen was last night, going aboard Preston's shark boat. I was on my way there next.'

'Right.' Thane swung into step beside him. 'Let's go – you can tell me about it on the way.'

'For a start, I went straight up to Oban after your call, and found Hollis's doctor.' Phil Moss gave an ironic grin. 'No aconite, Colin. Hollis had a heart condition which ruled it out.'

They walked on, Moss keeping up his summary in staccato style. Despite the doctor's depth-charge, he'd called next at Hollis's home – to be admitted by a very worried and elderly housekeeper who was trying to gather the resolution to go round to the police and report her employer missing.

'She didn't panic when Hollis failed to show up last night. It's happened before, when he's stayed on at the Isle or been held up by business. But with no word from him all day, she began to panic.'

'Check the house?'

'Uh-huh. A library crammed with books on ornithology, a showcase full of antiques, but no aconite in sight.'

They entered the harbour area, feet loud on the concrete causeway. Thane pointed ahead. 'Preston should be around – the *Rock Rose* is at her berth. Phil, how much do we know about Hollis's movements?'

'I've got some of Inspector Davidson's county men working on that now.' His companion hesitated. 'It's a funny thing, Colin, and maybe means nothing; but neither Preston's boat nor the *Gabrielle* have made a move all today.'

Funny, peculiar, agreed Thane. Unless both Sonders and Preston were waiting on something to happen, expecting and knowing it would occur sooner or later.

A record player was blaring aboard the *Rock Rose*, and the faint smell of cooking lingered in the air. They dropped down to the motor sailer's deck from the quayside, and almost instantly the music from the cabin stopped in mid-tune to be replaced by the sound of hurried movement. Finn Preston's bearded face pressed against the glass of one of the wheelhouse windows, and then the door was flung open.

'Back again?' There was a surly tension in his attitude.

'Some more questions, Mr Preston.' Thane threw the reply with equally brusque edge.

The shark-fisher gave a grunt. 'All right, come on down – and watch your head on the hatchway combing.'

They followed him down the short companionway ladder into the motor sailer's cabin, where Gwen Preston sat on one of the long day-couches, her feet on the cushions, her knees drawn up close to her chin.

Out of the working rig in which she'd been dressed on his first visit to the *Rock Rose*, Preston's wife was hardly recognizable. The tomboy jeans and floppy sweater had been discarded for dark blue slacks in tailored linen, a cream silk blouse with deeply veed neckline and a sharply contrasting flame-red neckerchief, knotted loosely at her throat. Lipstick, powder, and her long brunette hair brushed into a mass of darkly glowing glory completed the transformation. But, like her husband, Gwen Preston was on edge. It showed in the faint tightening on her lips as they entered, the strained deliberate way in which she rose to greet them.

'Drink, Chief Inspector?' Finn Preston raised a questioning eyebrow.

Thane shook his head. 'No thanks. Preston, was Edgar Hollis here last night?'

'Yes, he was. Why?' It was the girl who answered.

'Were you both here at the time?'

She nodded. Preston moved over beside her and gave a rumbling growl. 'Whatever this is, keep my wife out of it, Thane.'

'Can't be done.' The two men faced each other across the narrow cabin, Thane once again conscious of Finn Preston's towering bulk. In the background, Phil Moss let his right hand fall to his side, feeling the comforting shape of the sawn-off hardwood baton beneath the cloth of his jacket.

Gwen Preston broke the silence, turning to her husband, her face a study of controlled emotion. 'Hear him out, Finn. If he chooses, we've no option anyway.'

The bearded Viking chewed his lip, shrugged, and the crisis was over. 'As you say, lass. But answer me first, Chief Inspector. Why Hollis?'

'Because the man has disappeared.' Thane watched them closely, saw a quick glance pass between the couple, a glance which might almost have been taken as a sign of sudden relief.

'As far as we know, he hasn't been seen since last night, when he came aboard this boat.'

'Huh!' The shark-fisher gave a gurgling half-laugh. 'So you come here thinking we've tied him up and shoved him down in the bilges!' He moved over, took a cigarette from the packet lying on a porthole ledge, lit it, and grinned across at them. 'He was here all right – and I ended up shoving him back up on that quayside. Told him the next time he came back I'd stick a harpoon in where it would hurt most!'

'Mrs Preston?'

She nodded confirmation.

'What time did he leave?' Phil Moss had his notebook out, pencil ready.

'Dusk, around ten o'clock,' said the girl.

'What was the quarrel about?' Once again Thane saw a glance pass between Finn Preston and his wife, but this time it was one of mutual caution. 'Preston, this is a deadly serious matter – I want the truth.'

'Then I'll tell the truth, and no more.' The man sucked a deep lungful of smoke. 'He came to warn me off. Said that once the police left the Isle his precious Bird Society were putting another warden on duty out there, and that they'd prosecute if I even tried to land. We chased him off, and we haven't seen him since. Look, why bother us? Why not try your yachting pal Royan Sonders?'

'Sonders?'

'Uh-huh. They met on the quayside after Hollis left here, then went off together.' Preston was confident again, speaking with a new security.

Thane turned to the girl. 'Did you see this, Mrs Preston?'

She shook her head. 'No, I stayed below – but Finn told me at the time.'

Preston grimaced. 'Most of the other boats were out, and it was dusk. There might have been someone around, but that's your job, isn't it? I've told you my story, and if you don't believe it then it's up to you to prove I'm lying – not to me to prove I'm telling you the truth.'

'I'll believe you, Preston – as far as you've gone and for the moment.' Thane pursed his lips. 'We'll probably be back later, and I wouldn't advise you to leave harbour before morning.'

'Don't worry about that,' Preston assured him. 'We'll be here. Check on Royan Sonders, that's my advice.' He raised one hand in sardonic farewell as the two detectives turned to go.

Getting out to the *Gabrielle* at her off-shore mooring posed their next problem, but there was an interruption. As the two detectives clambered from the motor sailer's deck to the quayside a uniformed constable tramped purposefully towards them.

'Message from Inspector Davidson, sir,' he told Thane. 'We've found Hollis's car – it was left at the garage down the road yesterday morning, and he hasn't been back since. We've traced him to the Post Office, too, sir. He was there yesterday evening, just before it closed.'

'Which plugs another gap,' said Moss. 'The manager at the Inverlay Arms told me Hollis had dinner there last night and then waited around in the lounge for a spell before he went out.'

The constable hesitated. 'And there was a separate message, Mr Thane. Your wife telephoned the station and said it was important she contacted you.'

Thane frowned. Mary didn't telephone him in the middle of a case unless there was some urgency. But on those rare occasions, the message she left was usually explicit. It would have to wait. 'I'll take care of that later,' he thanked the county man. 'Tell Inspector Davidson I'm going to try to get out to the *Gabrielle* next.'

'If it's Mr Sonders you're looking for, sir, he's up at the hotel.' The uniformed man kept a straight face as he added, 'I thought I'd maybe find you in the bar, and looked in – I saw Mr Sonders there less than five minutes ago.'

Sonders was still in residence when they reached the Inverlay Arms. The bar counter was busy, but the South African yachtsman and two of his crew were at a table in a comparatively quiet corner of the room.

'I'd like to see you for a moment, alone,' Thane told him. Sonders nodded, murmured to the two seamen, then followed the detectives through to the privacy of the small, otherwise deserted residents' lounge.

'I told my men to wait for me,' he explained, settling into the nearest armchair. 'Now, Chief Inspector, how can I help you?'

Once again Thane used the direct approach. 'Edgar Hollis is missing, and I've been told you met him late last night.'

'Missing?' Sonders gave every sign of concern. 'You mean he may have had – well, a car accident?'

'Not a car accident, nor any other kind of accident that we know about,' said Thane quietly. 'Did you see him last night?'

'By pure chance, yes.' Sonders leaned forward in the chair. 'What are you trying to suggest?'

'All I'm trying to do is to find out what's happened to him.' Thane rubbed a thumb along his jawline, feeling the thickening stubble which was a reminder of his 6 a.m. start to the day. 'What happened when you met?'

'Well' – the paunchy South African frowned. 'We were on the quayside. Hollis was upset and more than a little angry because he had had a row with that lumbering oaf Preston. It seemed Preston had ended up threatening him – Hollis had warned Preston he was to stay clear of Sanctuary Isle.

'I thought the man was still pretty shaken, and besides, I wanted to talk to him. I took him in the runabout out to the *Gabrielle* and gave him a cup of coffee – he doesn't drink. We talked, and then I brought him ashore again, about 11 p.m.'

'To the quay?'

'Yes.' Sonders appeared a trifle uncomfortable. 'This is – difficult, especially in the circumstances. But Hollis told me he was going back to see Preston again. He'd left a package aboard when he was more or less tossed ashore, and he wanted to go back for it. I suggested he wait until the morning, but he wouldn't.' He shrugged. 'I thought of going with him, but if I'd turned up at the *Rock Rose* it would have been like a red rag to a bull. I said goodbye at the quayside, and went back to the *Gabrielle*.'

Phil Moss intervened. 'Did he say what was in the package?'

'No . . . I didn't ask, I'm afraid. But I gathered that it wasn't important, that Hollis was going back as a pure matter of principle.'

'Or stubbornness,' growled Thane. 'Mr Sonders, I'm duty-bound to ask you this. Did anyone see you bring Hollis ashore?'

The South African took the question calmly. 'It's possible. By then it was dark, of course, but I think – yes, one of the drift-net boats had just berthed. Chief Inspector, you've been aboard the *Gabrielle* once already – if it helps, I've no objection to a full search from stem to stern, this minute.'

If Sonders was involved in the Bird Society man's disappearance, then the offer was a bluff, a bluff built on the stonewall certainty that a search would yield nothing. Yet

87

there was also Tinemann's death, with its shadowy uncertain background. . . . Thane made up his mind. 'As pure routine, I'll accept. When do you plan to go aboard?'

'Now, if it suits.'

'Inspector Moss will go with you, and have a look around.' He got a faint tendril of amusement from the look of resignation which flicked across Phil Moss's already gloomy countenance. 'Mr Sonders, there's one thing I'd like to know. You said you'd wanted to talk to Hollis – what about?'

Sonders rose from his chair. 'Sanctuary Isle, Mr Thane. The Society's work impresses me. I told him I proposed to make a donation to their funds for the specific purpose of helping to establish the bird sanctuary's funds on a firm basis. I posted my cheque for £1,000 to their chairman this morning.

'Ready, Mr Moss?'


Once the South African had left, Phil Moss by his side, the two deck hands tagging a few paces to the rear, Thane walked along to the village police station. Inspector Davidson, a telephone to one ear, waved a brief greeting and mimed towards the chair opposite him. The office seemed more crowded with furniture than previously, and it was a moment or two before he realized the reason. The table and other equipment which made up their temporary 'C.I.D. room' in the station's single cell had been dragged out from there, and the cell's solid one-piece door was closed and locked.

Davidson, his conversation finished, put down the telephone. 'Another line on Hollis,' he said briskly. 'I located his office clerk, a fellow called Lattan. Hollis had an appointment with a client for ten this morning. They were to meet in Hollis's office at Oban, with an important piece of business to discuss. Hollis phoned Lattan from here a little before six last night to double-check that all the necessary papers would be ready.'

'So at that time, anyway, he wasn't thinking of departing from routine.' Thane perched himself on the desk-edge. 'I see we've been evicted – got a customer inside?'

Purring satisfaction in his manner, the Argyll officer gave a slow nod. 'MacPherson the boatman. He was picked up a couple of hours ago.'

'What's the charge?'

'Breach of the peace and damaging police property. He sold his story to the *Daily Disc* last night for fifty pounds, and then promptly gave a different version to the *Glasgow Courier* for another thirty. The *Disc* man saw him this evening, and kicked up a row. MacPherson threw him into the harbour – and then when Sergeant Stewart came along and warned him, he knocked Stewart's hat into the water.'

Thane suppressed a grin. 'Drunk?'

'No more than usual.' Davidson's face mottled with suppressed fury. 'MacPherson seems to consider that he should be a law unto himself – but he's going to learn different before he's much older, I'll guarantee it.'

'I've seen Royan Sonders.' Thane eased himself into a more comfortable position on the desk-edge. 'He claims that the last he saw of Hollis, he was setting off to pay a return visit to the *Rock Rose*. There may be witnesses, the crew of a fishing boat that had just come into harbour.'

Davidson looked around the office and gave a sigh. Only one uniformed man remained – he had two still on duty out at the Isle, and the search had already consumed almost every other man in the tiny force he'd been able to scrape together from the corners of the divisional area. He reached for his hat, brushed a speck of lint from the black-and-white diced cap band round it, and the silver of the badge glinted in the light. 'I'll do it myself.' The hat rammed on his head, he strode out of the police station.

The telephone on the desk tempted Thane to make his promised call home. He reached out, then changed his mind.

'Constable!'

'Sir?' The policeman crossed towards him.

'What size of a staff is there at the village post office?'

'Just old Tom Watson the postmaster and his wife, Chief Inspector. They live in the house beside it.'

'None of our people have spoken to them yet?'

The constable shook his head. 'Haven't had a chance, sir, being so short of men.'

Thane swung off the desk, decision taken. 'If Inspector Moss gets back before I do, tell him to wait here.'

Inverlay's post office, one half of a long, low-roofed cottage with whitewashed stone walls, lay about 200 yards along the road from the police station. Red-painted window boxes graced its sills, bright with a mixture of marigolds and hyacinths. The postmaster's living quarters occupied the right-hand portion of the cottage, and Thane rapped twice on the iron knocker. After a brief wait, the door opened.

'Yes?' The woman, in her late forties, was plump and grey-haired.

'Mrs Watson? My name's Thane, I'm a police officer.'

She beckoned him in. 'You'll be the one down from Glasgow about Captain Tinemann being killed. Then there's another one with you, a thin miserable-looking soul.'

Phil Moss would hardly have appreciated the description. Thane followed the postmaster's wife into what was obviously their best room, a place dominated by dark, heavy Victorian furniture, every spare inch of shelf crammed with a miscellany of china ornaments, the window curtains thick brown velvet.

'Sit down,' she invited. 'If it's my husband you came to see I'm afraid he's out – away helping his brother at a calling on his farm. But maybe I can help?'

Gingerly, Thane lowered himself on to the hard stuffing of a straight-backed chair. 'You may be able to, Mrs Watson. Do you know a Mr Hollis?'

'Och goodness, I knew this would be happening,' sighed

the woman. 'I told Tom that the right thing to do was to tell the police when it came yesterday morning.'

'When – what came?' The chair creaked a little as he leaned forward.

'The parcel, of course,' she told him, mildly exasperated. 'The one that came in the post yesterday morning addressed to Captain Tinemann. Tom said – well, anyway Mr Thane, we asked Mr Hollis about it when he came in to make a phone call from the box. He said that as the parcel was addressed to an employee of the Bird Society he'd take it and tell you about it if necessary. You see, we sometimes get mail for the Bird Society addressed to Sanctuary Isle, and we just keep it until Mr Hollis looks in – though any letters that came for Captain Tinemann used to be taken out to him by Willie the boatman whenever he was making a trip.'

Thane gulped. 'This parcel – do you know what was in it?'

The postmaster's wife gave a sniff. 'Looking inside people's private mail would be a breach of the Post Office regulations. But I can tell you where it came from, if that helps. The parcel came C.O.D. – you know, cash on delivery. There was two pounds fourteen shillings to pay, and Mr Hollis gave me the money. I'll have the details on our copy of the receipt form.'

She left him, and returned within a couple of minutes carrying a thin, soft-covered ledger. 'Here it is, Mr Thane. Two pounds fourteen paid cash on delivery. I – I hope there's not going to be trouble over this.'

'Not as far as you're concerned, Mrs Watson.' He checked the entry. The amount was to be forwarded to a London firm, Messrs Davis Dewey, Marine Booksellers, Great Portland Street, W.1.

A copy of the receipt form's details in his notebook, he left the cottage and returned to the police station. Davidson was back, and the Argyll inspector appeared mildly satisfied. 'I think I've found your fishing boat,' he told Thane. 'It's almost definitely the *Lenore Glen* – she came in about that time last night, and she should be back in harbour again in about half an hour. I've got Sergeant Stewart waiting on her coming in.'

'Good. Any sign of Inspector Moss yet?'

Davidson shook his head. 'No, but the duty man took two calls while you were out. You've to contact Chief Superintendent Ilford in Glasgow, and your wife telephoned again.'

What on earth did Mary want? He finger-tapped the desk, then lifted the telephone and put in a call to Headquarters.

When Buddha Ilford's voice came on the line, the city C.I.D. boss was in a mood of growling pleasantry. 'Still enjoying the sea air, Colin? I've got some word back from Interpol – your query on Sonders' crew.'

'Good or bad, sir?'

'Good for you, maybe bad for Sonders. The *Gabrielle's* former crew were paid off when the yacht was laid up. Sonders moved his own men aboard when he took over. French section of Interpol say the names and descriptions we sent match up with a quartet of strong-arm boys from the Marseilles area – none of them wanted on any charge, but two have records and the other two should have. Petty stuff mainly, assault, smuggling, that sort of thing. The seafaring background is genuine enough, except that there's not a French shipping agent who'd touch any of 'em with a barge-pole. How's it going at your end – any line on this fellow Hollis?'

'Not so far,' Thane told him. 'But all the signs are that something pretty nasty has happened to him.'

Ilford gave a grunt. 'I hope not. The Chief Constable's beginning to take rather an interest in what's going on. The chairman of this ruddy Bird Society is a pal of his, and is starting to put on pressure. Well, I'm going home now – give me a call in the morning.'

Thane replaced the receiver with gentle care. So on one count anyway Sonders had lied – when he claimed that he had 'inherited' the *Gabrielle's* crew from the yacht's previous owner. In itself it wasn't a crime. But there had to be a reason for the lie, a reason which might cover other items.

Now Mary – he lifted the phone, gave the operator his home number, and pondered on the situation while he waited for the connection. Sonders had still told him about the package, while Finn Preston had made no mention of it. Yet if it had been left aboard, Preston or his wife must have found it. If Hollis had come back from his trip to the *Gabrielle*, and then gone over to Preston's boat to collect . . . he abandoned the tangle of possibilities as his wife's voice came on the line.

'Mary, it's Colin. What's up?'

Her sigh of relief came loud along the wire. 'Thank goodness – I was going to give you another ten minutes, then try again.'

'Something wrong with the kids?'

'No, nothing. But Colin, listen for a minute.' She was eager, and a little excited. 'You remember telling me about the arithmetic problem you found on a piece of paper, the one that had figures around it which didn't make sense?'

'Uh-huh. What about them?'

'Tommy was going to say something to you, and we told him to keep quiet –'

'Mary what the devil is this all about?' He tried to keep his exasperation to a minimum.

'Give me the figures again – just the two you mentioned.'

'One thousand five fifty-six, one thousand five eight-eight,' he told her. 'What about them?'

She chuckled. 'We've another detective in the family. They're not figures – they're dates. Tommy spotted it, and kept on at me after you'd gone. I thought he was just blethering until he showed me his history book.'

'For the love of – look, Mary, what dates?' He ignored Inspector Davidson's frankly curious stare, took only vague notice of the fact that Phil Moss had just entered the police office and was approaching.

93

'Fifteen eighty-eight, the Spanish Armada. The Spanish king at the time was Philip the Second, who reigned from 1556 to 1598. Colin – Colin, are you still there?'

'Yes.' Thane gave a faint groan while his imagination galloped along an entirely new pathway, fantastic in its implications.

'Does it help?' asked his wife hopefully. 'I felt it could be important.'

'If – yes, I think it does. I'll let you know.' He said goodbye, put down the phone, and drew one hand across his forehead. 'Somebody give me a cigarette!'

Phil Moss obliged, and supplied a light. 'The *Gabrielle's* clean as a whistle, Colin . . . or seems to be. What's up, trouble at home?'

Thane took a long drag on the cigarette. 'No, just some expert advice from a ten-year-old. Where can I get a history book, a good one?'

Inspector Davidson looked at him goggle-eyed. 'A what?'

'A history book,' snapped Thane. 'One with a large-sized chapter on the Spanish Armada. And don't look at me like that. I haven't gone crazy!'

The county officer scratched his head. 'The schoolmaster might be your best bet. I'll go along and try him if you like.'

'One other thing.' Thane jerked a thumb in the direction of the station cell. 'I want you to turn our friend Willie loose.'

'MacPherson?' Davidson was indignant. 'I can't do that – he's cautioned and charged, and he's due up in court in the morning.'

'I mean it.' Thane's manner hardened perceptibly. 'I'm not trying to pull rank on you, Davidson – but I'm here to run a murder investigation, maybe a double murder investigation. I'm not interested in any local feuds, no matter how justified. I want MacPherson out of that cell, even if it means going right to the top. If there are any comebacks, I'll take the burden.'

The county officer gave in with scant grace. He rose, rammed his hat back on his head, and nodded across to the duty constable. 'You heard, let him out. I'll go and get this history book, whatever good it will do.'

As the street door crashed shut behind the man, Phil Moss gave a low whistle. 'I'd say he wasn't pleased.'

'Can't say I blame him,' shrugged Thane. 'I don't like strangers messing around my backyard, so why should he feel any different?'

There was a rattle and click as the duty constable unlocked the cell door and swung it open.

'Playing a hunch?' queried Moss.

Thane nodded, then his expression changed to a grin as Willie MacPherson emerged from his enforced lodging. The boatman was in dinner jacket and full evening dress, complete with wine-coloured cummerbund.

'Going somewhere, Willie?'

'I should be playing in the dance band right now,' protested the boatman. 'Och, I didn't mean to knock the sergeant's cap into the water – it was just that the temptation was too much.'

'And the reporter?' queried Moss.

'Well, that takes a wee bit explaining,' began the boatman.

Thane cut him short. 'Another time, Willie. Inspector Davidson's agreed to drop the charges, provided you give me some help in return.'

MacPherson gave a wry glance towards the waiting cell. 'Name what you want,' he invited.

'For a start, an introduction to your mother as being a policeman who has done you a good turn,' Thane told him. 'Since you landed in that cell one or two things have been happening. The first is that Edgar Hollis is missing. Did you see him around yesterday?'

'Missing?' The boatman's mouth fell open. 'I saw him, och, it would be coming on for nine o'clock last night. He was walking down towards the harbour.'

'You didn't see him after that?'

95

The boatman was positive. 'No, because I was on my way home then. I remember wondering what was in the wee parcel he had under his arm, but he just gave me a "hello" and walked past without stopping.' He looked up as Inspector Davidson marched back into the police office. 'Hey, Inspector, I'm out!'

The county officer ignored him, and thumped a large cloth-bound volume on the desk before Thane. 'Your history book. I still don't know what this is all about, but I'll carry my share of any troubles going.' His temper had cooled, his manner was now resigned bewilderment. 'What's the angle? Not the Tobermory treasure galleon?'

'Maybe. I'm not sure myself.' Thane was already flipping the pages of the book, seeking the section he required. He located it at last and began reading, Phil Moss looking over his shoulder.

The Armada story was a schoolboy classic, the peak of the high romance of Elizabethan times, of Sir Francis Drake, Frobisher, Hawkins, and other piratical patriots. One hundred and thirty Spanish ships, carrying 30,000 men, had set out to conquer England and instead had been harried, burned and smashed by the mosquito-stab attacks of the smaller, lighter-gunned English ships. Finally, they had fled, many galleons steering north, preferring the sea-hazards of the long voyage round the north of Scotland to the short but cannon-bristling gauntlet they would have to run on any return voyage through the narrow English Channel.

The date, 1588. Thane tapped the next paragraph with his forefinger.

'This is the kernel of it, Phil. The north was swept by gales that year, nineteen galleons are known to have been wrecked on the coasts of Scotland and Ireland, and a whole lot more simply disappeared under the waves. Then there was the Tobermory galleon, the vessel supposed to be the Armada's payship.'

'But that's a long way from here,' protested Inspector Davidson. 'Take a look at the map' – he unfolded the station's Ordnance Survey sheet, and spread it on the desk. 'We're here. The island of Mull is on the other side of the Firth of Lorne – and remember, we see only the south-east tip. The town of Tobermory is at the northern end, and that's almost forty miles away by sea. Besides, the Tobermory galleon's location is known – divers have been trying to get down through the mud to it for years.'

The history book gave that, too. There were various differences in detail, but all the main points in the assorted tales agreed – as did the mighty authority of the official State Documents of Scotland and the equally authentic and ancient records of the Clan MacLean, which had then held power throughout the area.

Gale-battered, short of provisions, the Spanish galleon had taken refuge in Tobermory harbour. When its captain wanted stores, the MacLean chief agreed with the proviso that the Spaniards helped him mop up one or two local enemies. The captain agreed, the unfortunate neighbours were subdued, and stores were loaded aboard the galleon. Just as the ship was about to sail, the MacLean chief demanded payment for goods supplied, and was forcefully told by the Spaniards that their services had already squared the account. The MacLeans were angry, and a little later, just as she was about to sail, the ship blew up – taking with her nearly five hundred Spaniards. One story was that a MacLean retainer had laid a trail of gunpowder to the ship's magazine and lit it, another that it was the work of an English spy. The result was the same either way . . . the galleon went straight down, to lie buried in thick off-shore mud and silt.'

'Colin, are you trying to suggest' – Phil Moss had an unbending faith in the Millside C.I.D. chief, but for once even he was openly sceptical. 'Tobermory is a long way away, as Davidson says. What's it got to do with Tinemann, or Hollis if it comes to that?'

Thane looked up at a circle of frowning faces. 'I'm going to do some folklore research,' he said calmly. 'Ready, Willie?'

The MacPherson home was a small crofter cottage clinging to the scanty shelter of a hollow high on the hillside above the village. The police Jaguar bumped over a rough track for about a mile in protesting bottom gear, then stopped a few yards from the little heather-thatched house.

Willie MacPherson led the way to the low-set door, Thane and Moss following – Davidson had decided to remain with what he considered the more practical business of questioning the crew of the fishing boat when it reached harbour.

The boatman threw open the croft door and gave a piercing whistle.

'Hey, mother! Your son is home – and I've got the polis wi' me!'

From inside the house there was a muffled exclamation followed by a massive clatter of pots and pans. A shrill voice was raised in what Thane imagined must be an unusually pungent outburst in the native Gaelic tongue, and the grin on Willie MacPherson's face as he listened decided him against asking for an English translation.

A small plump figure bustled through. Mrs MacPherson had a white apron tied round her middle, was dressed in a knitted wool dress of doubtful vintage, and had a light of battle in her deep-set pale blue eyes.

'Whateffer it is, Willie, say nothing till we haff got the lawyer down from Oban –'

'Och, I'm not in trouble this time,' soothed her son. 'At least I was but I'm not, if you know what I mean.'

'Then why are you not playing at the dance?' she skirled. 'Dressed up there like a bantam rooster looking for a midden! And who are these two anyway? They are not Davidson's men.'

MacPherson handled the introductions. 'The big one is Chief Inspector Thane, and the wee one is Inspector Moss, the ones I told you about, up from the city to find out who killed Captain Tinemann.'

'Humph.' She looked them up and down. 'They haff

98

been taking their time about it, too, from all accounts. Well, come inside.'

Meekly, they followed her through the short dark hallway and into the big, airy kitchen beyond, a room which obviously served for living, eating and cooking combined. Sparkling clean throughout, burnished metal pots gleaming on their hooks, a peat fire flickering its slow-burning flame in the black iron grate, it made a homely setting – and was not quite what Thane had expected.

'Now then, you – the tall one – what hass Willie been up to this time?' she demanded. 'Not that he iss admitting anything, mind you, just that I want to know.'

'I was able to help him out of a little spot of bother,' said Thane, going over and standing with his back to the fire. 'It's over and done with, whatever happens. But you might be able to help me, Mrs MacPherson; help me solve a murder.'

'Me? You're havering!'

Her son shook his head. 'He means it, mother – something to do with the folk-tales, though I haven't understood why myself yet.'

'Well, well.' She was immediately interested. 'First, you'll be having a wee drink – and no nonsense about being on duty. Eh, Willie' – she glanced anxiously towards her son.

'The good stuff, mother,' he assured her. 'Not the bottle with the label. The Chief Inspector won't be saying anything about it when he gets back.'

'Hmm.' Mrs MacPherson was still cautious. 'Well, if you're sure.' From a cupboard she brought out four tumblers, and then, after another brief hesitation, she went over to the bundle of peats beside the fireside, lifted the top one, and pulled out a bottle from the hollow space within. Three generous measures of the light-brown liquid gurgled into the tumblers, then, as she moved to the last of the glasses, Phil Moss cleared his throat apologetically.

'Not for me, Mrs MacPherson.'

'Oh! Why not? This iss not the rubbish you'll be getting

in your city bars, policeman. This iss genuine triple-run spirit, made – eh – by a friend of ours.'

'I can't drink whisky,' explained the detective. 'I've a bad stomach.'

'Och well.' Mrs MacPherson corked the bottle and returned it to the hiding-place. 'Slainch!' She lifted the nearest glass and drank.

'Slainch!' Her son followed suit.

'Cheers!' Thane lifted his glass and took a sip. Fire raced in his throat, then flowed through him. He gave a splutter. 'Strong stuff.'

'At first yes, but clean as the mountain dew, Chief Inspector.' Mrs MacPherson took another gulp, then put down her empty tumbler. 'Now, what iss it you want?'

Thane took another cautious sip, felt the fire race again, but this time decided the feeling was not wholly unpleasant. 'You know most of the stories of the old days in these parts, Mrs MacPherson. I mean the real stories – this is important, and I don't want you to make up a tale just to please me.'

The pale blue eyes twinkled. 'You did Willie a favour, Chief Inspector. Whateffer I tell you will be as it was told to me, passed down in our family. But they're the old stories, remember . . . I can't be saying they're true.'

Thane laid down his glass. 'How did Sanctuary Isle get its name?'

She frowned. 'That iss a strange thing to be asking, and you – aye, you the first to ask me it for many a year. It iss an old, old name, Chief Inspector, not as old as the Gaelic, but one which became used in time.' Moving almost by reflex, she went over to the peats, took out the bottle, and poured a slightly smaller measure into her glass. 'My mother's mother told me – och, no, that's a lie for a start. It wass in an old history of the parish we had at home, written by a minister long dead and buried by then. The tale wass that some foreigners had their ship wrecked in a big storm in the Firth, and were saved by managing to get to the island. They came ashore here afterwards, and

100

some ended up being put to the claymore, being almost as quarrelsome as their hosts. But the foreigners called the Isle their sanctuary from the storm – and the name stuck.'

'What type of foreigners?' Thane felt a sudden tension.

'Och, Spaniards, the story went. Some of them that were in the Armada.'

Behind him, Phil Moss gave a quiet gurgle. Thane's mind froze solid. He took a long swallow from the tumbler of triple-run whisky – and the fire brought sudden tears to his eyes at the same time as it rapid-thawed his thinking.

Willie MacPherson had a doubting expression on his face. 'You haven't told that story before, mother.'

'Nobody's asked me,' she snapped back. 'Not since you were a bairn, anyway.'

'All right, mother.' The boatman chewed thoughtfully on his lower lip. 'Then that is the truth of it as far as we know, Chief Inspector – though the old stories cannot always be trusted.'

He saw them to the door of the cottage and across towards the waiting car. 'Chief Inspector. . . .' Hands in his pockets, MacPherson frowned down at the dusty track. 'I would not like to be getting a friend of mine into trouble, especially when I believe he has done no real wrong, but – do you think that harmless wee man Hollis is dead?'

Thane paused, one hand on the car door. 'Until we've found his body, nothing is certain. But if you've anything to tell me, you'd better get it off your chest now, when it may help.'

MacPherson gave a shrug. 'The first part's easy enough, little more than a tale I heard from some of the fishermen down at the harbour – it's just with you being so interested in the Isle. Two or three weeks ago it was, when one of the Inverlay boats was coming back from the fishing grounds late one night. They were sure they saw some lights on the Isle – and no-one on it at the time. There was only a flicker or two, and it was a calm night. The boat went in a bit closer, and they gave a hail, just in case some other boat was in trouble. But there was no reply, and they decided that the look-out had been seeing things, maybe a light from one of the mainland houses.'

'Two or three weeks ago,' mused Thane. 'Before the Bird Society put Tinemann on the Isle as warden?'

'Aye.' MacPherson grinned sheepishly. 'As for the other thing, it's that I was a bit absent-minded when you asked me something the other day – about whether I told anyone that the captain had run out of whisky and that I'd have to be taking him out more. Eh . . . I did tell one person, Mr Thane, just a mention when I saw her.'

'Her?'

The boatman nodded. 'Finn Preston's wife. But the Prestons wouldn't have anything to do with the murder, Mr Thane – Captain Tinemann was a friend, wasn't he?'

Thane refused to be drawn. 'We'll see, Willie. It's a pity you didn't – remember – earlier.' He gave the boatman a hard, unblinking stare. 'I'd hate to hear of you selling any more stories to reporters, particularly about what's happened this evening. Understand this, Willie. If you do, I'll find out – and before I'm done with you I'll hand you your guts for a boat-rope.'

MacPherson shuffled his feet. 'You have my solemn word on it, Chief Inspector.'

As the car bumped on its slow return journey to the village below, Phil Moss swallowed a couple of pills and cursed all Highland boatmen. 'If Gwen Preston knew, then her husband almost certainly knew too,' he growled. 'Which makes quite a difference.'

'Puts him practically in the clear as far as Tinemann is concerned.' Thane was equally irritated. 'Lord preserve us from characters who try hard to help their friends – they practically weave a rope for the hangman. If Preston knew about the liquor shortage and that MacPherson was going out again to the Isle the next day, then he wouldn't have gone to all the trouble put into Tinemann's murder. Whoever did it thought it would be about a week before the body was found – and was banking on it being tagged a natural death. I wonder – just what did he plan to do in that week?'

His second-in-command gave a grunt. 'You've done everything so far but name it, Colin – look around for bits of a Spanish galleon and what it was carrying. But what have you got to go on? Be honest. As a motive for murder, this galleon idea has more holes in it than – than one of these ruddy fishing nets.'

'Maybe, maybe not, Phil. There was that piece of old wood hidden in the store shed, then the dates we found on the slip of paper – and I'm prepared to bet that we find the parcel from London was a book or books on the Armada. Look, supposing Tinemann had found something while patrolling the Isle, a coin perhaps. Wouldn't it be commonsense that he'd want to know the exact year of the Armada, so that he could be sure the coin or whatever the blazes it was could have come from an Armada ship?'

Unconvinced, his friend gave a sigh. 'I've read newspaper stories about the Tobermory galleon, and how the navy, private enterprise outfits and all the rest have tried to get down to it. And that there may have been plenty of cash aboard when it was blown up. But even there, Colin, where they know they've located a ruddy galleon, would it be worth one, maybe two murders?'

The Jaguar reached the end of the track, slid into higher gear as its wheels met the smooth tarmac road leading to Inverlay, and purred happily.

'Some people might think so,' said Thane, reaching into his pocket. 'The Tobermory galleon is believed to have been called the *Florentia* – one story is that she was carrying the equivalent of £30,000,000 in gold and gems. Cigarette, Phil?'

Detective Inspector Moss had absolutely nothing to say.

\* \* \*

Dusk was merging with early dark when the car reached Inverlay police station, and the first stabbing beams were already sweeping across the water from the automatic lighthouse on Sanctuary Isle. Inside the police station, blinds were drawn and electric lights glowed down.

Inspector Davidson met them as they entered, and the county man, a self-righteous air about him, came straight out with his news. 'While you've been gone' – on a wild goose chase, his meaning was clear – 'Sergeant Stewart and I met that fishing boat I mentioned. I brought the skipper back with me, and you'll find him interesting.'

He led them behind the office counter and over to where the man was waiting. 'Skipper Gault, of the *Lenore Glen*,' introduced Davidson. The fisherman, sturdily built, bald, weatherbeaten, still in his working rig of Government surplus battle-dress dyed dark blue, gave them a brief nod.

Phil Moss took out his notebook and pencil and stood ready. 'Thanks for waiting, skipper,' said Thane. 'Inspector Davidson will have told you already what we're trying to find out. For a start, what time did your boat get in last night?'

''Bout eleven,' answered the fisherman laconically. 'Bit later than usual – we'd an engine fault.'

'Do you know a man called Hollis?'

'The Bird Society fellow,' he agreed. 'I've seen him a few times around the harbour. Saw him last night, too – Inspector Davidson asked me that right off. Happened just after we tied up at the quay. I was on the quayside with one of m' crew, getting ready to unload the catch, when we heard that wee speedboat coming in from the *Gabrielle*. It stopped by the stone steps, and Hollis came ashore. By then it was pretty dark, of course, but I think it was Sonders, the *Gabrielle's* owner, who was with him.' He stopped, waiting for the next question. Met by silence, he gave a faint shrug and went on. 'That was about all there was to it. We heard 'em say good night, then Hollis came up the steps and walked past us. The speedboat turned and headed back to the yacht.'

'And Hollis?'

The fishing boat skipper wiped one hand across his nose. 'Like I said, he walked past us – I said good night, and he gave me a nod.'

'Was he carrying anything – a parcel?' probed Thane.

'Nope.'

'Which way was he heading?'

The man stirred restlessly. 'Up towards the village, where else?'

'And your boat – was it moored nearer the harbour mouth than the *Rock Rose*? Would Hollis have to pass the *Rock Rose* to get to the village?'

'Preston's boat?' The fisherman frowned. 'Aye, he'd pass her on the way.'

Thane felt suddenly disheartened. If Sonders had put Hollis ashore – 'You said it was dark. What makes you so sure it was Hollis who passed you?'

'It was Hollis,' growled the fisherman. 'I heard his name when he and Sonders were saying good night – and I saw his face as he went past. There was enough light coming from my own boat to make that plain to see.'

'Did you see him go aboard Preston's boat?'

The fisherman shook his head. 'Look, mister, we'd work to do while this was going on, and he just moved off into the darkness.'

Once Skipper Gault had left, on his way back to the *Lenore Glen*, Thane had only one wish – to be alone for a spell, to try to reconcile fact and theory, proof and probability.

Inspector Davidson had other ideas. 'Well, do we go and collect Preston?' he demanded.

'On what charge?' asked Thane wearily. 'That he might have done it?'

Phil Moss gave a growl of agreement. 'We'd look dam' silly if we tossed him in a cell and then Edgar Hollis walked in that door first thing tomorrow morning. All right, it's unlikely, but that sort of thing has happened before.' He slumped down on a chair beside Thane, gave a grimace at life in general, then posed his own question. 'But Davidson's got a point – what do we do now?'

There was a blotting pad on the desk, and a ball-point pen lying handy. Slowly, carefully, Thane began a doodling outline, gradually emerging as a cartoon whale chasing a galleon, chased in turn by a giant-sized seagull. 'First, we keep an eye on Preston but otherwise leave him alone. Second, Phil, you contact that London bookshop first thing tomorrow and find out what was in the package they sent to Captain Tinemann. Third, we let Royan Sonders set off for Switzerland tomorrow as planned. Fourth' – he stopped the doodle, drew a line through it, and gave a tight grin, 'I'm going to phone Buddha Ilford, and ask him to contact Interpol. I want Sonders followed – until my own plane gets there.'

Inspector Davidson swallowed hard. 'You mean – you're going off to Switzerland and leaving things here as they are?'

'Not quite,' corrected Thane. 'I want you to withdraw your guard from Sanctuary Isle, and make it known. Use the excuse you're short of men, and need them elsewhere – that's genuine enough, anyway. There are a couple of other minor matters, but Inspector Moss can handle them.' He rose to his feet. 'Well, I'm calling it a day. I'll phone Buddha Ilford from the hotel – once I've worked out the best way to persuade him I'm not completely crazy. Good night.'

He went out alone. In the quiet of the police office, Inspector Davidson's fingers drummed loud on the desk. Then, despairingly, he appealed to Phil Moss. 'Is he always like this?'

'Always,' said Moss – and tried to appear cheerful.

# Chapter Five

A shadowing detail, airline style, has one basic advantage. Once the man you are trailing boards a plane and that plane takes off, it is more than a little difficult for him to leave until the aircraft reaches its destination. Again, there is a distinct difference between lounging back in cosseted air-conditioned comfort and standing in even the most sheltered of doorways.

In a British European Airways jet Comet high above cloud-covered Central France, Colin Thane allowed himself the luxury of a quiet snooze. Winning Buddha Ilford round to his viewpoint had not been easy, but once that had been achieved and details settled, all that the Millside divisional chief had to do was surrender himself to a smooth-running process of organization.

Royan Sonders left Inverlay by hired car at 5 a.m. and arrived at Renfrew Airport, Glasgow, in ample time to take his seat aboard the 8 a.m. flight to London. The next London flight left half an hour later, with Chief Detective Inspector Thane as a late addition to its passenger list. When Thane's plane landed at London, his quarry was conveniently engaged at the Swissair ticket desk where an apologetic official took just long enough to sort out an imaginary seating difficulty to allow the detective to be met and whisked to the shelter of the airport's security office.

Flight SR 111, the Swissair Caravelle jet flight to Zurich, left on schedule at 10.55 a.m. with Sonders aboard. As the plane climbed skywards, Colin Thane emerged from the security office with ample time in hand to stroll the distance to where passengers were assembling for his flight, the 11.15 a.m. B.E.A. Comet to the same destination.

The Swissair Caravelle touched down at Zurich airport at 12.20 p.m. Twenty minutes later, at 12.40, the B.E.A. Comet whined in to land. There was a trace of rain, and the sky above was dull as the Comet passengers crossed to the terminal building and the brisk formalities of Customs and Immigration. The polite blue-uniformed official who glanced at Thane's passport gave a faint smile and signalled to a fat cheerful individual lounging nearby. The man concerned removed a long rope-like cigar from his mouth and came over.

'Herr Thane? Kriminalinspektor Bremse.' They shook hands, the Swiss policeman returned the cigar to his mouth, and gestured towards the exit door. 'Your man is quite safe, Herr Thane, but I would prefer . . .'

Thane nodded. 'Whatever you've arranged suits me.'

'Good.' Bremse took an envelope from his inside pocket and handed it over. 'This has come for you.'

The telegram inside was suitably terse. 'HOLLIS BODY RECOVERED FROM WATER OUTSIDE HARBOUR. SKULL FRACTURED. MACMASTER P.M.ING+MOSS.' Thane folded the message-form and returned it to the envelope.

'Does it change your plans?' queried the Swiss.

'Makes them more important,' said Thane grimly.

'Then I have a car outside.' Bremse led the way through the bustle of the terminal building to the car park beyond and ushered Thane into the passenger seat of a black, dusty Volkswagen saloon. The Swiss slid behind the steering wheel, flicked the switch of the car's two-way radio and, as the set hummed to life, picked up the hand microphone. He spoke a few words into the instrument, received an immediate crackling acknowledgment, and was satisfied. The microphone went back on to its hook, he started the Volkswagen's engine, and the car drew away.

'All is in order,' he declared. 'I have two units watching. Your Afrikaner is on the Lucerne road, a journey of about an hour – but I think we will have until tonight before he moves.'

Plump, medium height, with a baggy-kneed blue suit, faded red tie and a pink, almost baby-smooth complexion, the Swiss detective relaxed happily behind the wheel. His command of English was faultless with a minimum undertone of accent – Thane thought guiltily of the mass of Britons who descended on the Continent convinced that a loud voice and a travellers' chequebook were all they required to move around, and to hell with exploring the other man's language.

'What's the set-up?' he queried.

'Set-up?' Bremse was momentarily puzzled. 'Ah . . . I am with you. When Interpol passed on your request, we made what my American friends call the "stake-out." Switzerland is a small country, Herr Thane, only about half the size of your Scotland. Sometimes that helps. I find that your Sonders has arranged a self-drive hire car to wait him at Zurich airport, booked for today only. He has a reservation on the night flight back to London, again in his own name. So I say to myself, "Bremse, this Sonders is here on legitimate business – or that is his story. He would be foolish to depart from that by using another name."' The Volkswagen dropped down a gear and swept past a long, heavily-loaded lorry and trailer, then tucked in behind a fast-moving touring bus packed with holiday-makers.

'Then I decided that if I wanted to make quite sure I would not be followed, I might have a second car waiting somewhere.' He removed the cigar from his mouth and waved it for emphasis. 'Your Afrikaner has done just that. A second car has been hired in his name from a garage in Lucerne, for this evening only. Now, my friend, have you been in our country before?'

Thane considered his companion with new respect. 'Only once, on my honeymoon. We stayed at a hotel at Interlaken – a two-week travel agency tour. So by your reckoning Sonders won't make a step out of line until he switches cars?'

Bremse gave a nod. 'And until then, my men will keep watch. They will make very sure they are not seen – most of them have put on too much weight to want to return to uniform.'

The threatened rain broke into a drenching downpour a few kilometres before they reached Lucerne, and Bremse gave a grumble of disappointment. 'A pity. On this road on a clear day, the view – well, it is magnificent.'

'It happens with me, too,' sympathized Thane. 'Every time I take a visitor to see Loch Lomond, there's either a mist or a howling gale.'

The car radio crackled another brief message, and the Swiss detective acknowledged.

'It is as I expected,' he beamed. 'Your Sonders has stopped in Lucerne. At the moment, he is about to have lunch with some eminently respectable finance house representatives. In Switzerland, the matter of eating is treated with respect – it will be probably two hours before they finish. Herr Thane, I think we should follow their example.'

Kriminalinspektor Bremse piloted the Volkswagen close in to the centre of the city, parked with authoritative disregard for official signposts, gave his location to the radio control point, then led the way to his favourite restaurant.

The meal was massive, almost overpowering in quantity of helpings. Napkin under his chin in true trencherman style, Bremse took the menu in his stride, starting off with a thick soup, ladled liberally from a massive tureen; tackling a mountainous quantity of Berner Platte – smoked meats served with sauerkraut and vegetables – washed it down with a tankard of beer, enjoyed a cream-laced fruit salad and then called for coffee.

Thane surrendered even before the sweet. He settled for coffee, sat back, lit a cigarette, and decided that a Swiss restaurant transported to Scotland would make an over-night fortune.

110

'No liqueur?' The Swiss appeared disappointed. 'Ah well, there is work ahead – perhaps you are right.'

At three-thirty they went back to the car and Bremse checked with radio control. Sonders had left his companions ten minutes previously, and was now apparently killing time. He visited a bank, went from there to a coffee-house, and then spent some time browsing over a book-shop's display.

In the Volkswagen the air grew thick and pungent as the Swiss policeman lit yet another of his long cigars. At last, at four-thirty, the radio gave the message they'd been waiting for – Sonders had returned to his car.

'Now,' mused Bremse, 'my boys have a little diversion ahead – Herr Sonders makes sure no one is on his heels.'

He was right. Royan Sonders spent the next twenty minutes, in a twisting, doubling journey round the city and its suburbs, tracked by a monotonous flow of reports over the radio. The Swiss inspector's face creased with humour. 'Perhaps I should admit it,' he confessed. 'My boys are not far behind him, but I also arranged for a' –he snapped his fingers – 'a homer tube, I think you call it, to be fitted to his car.'

Thane nodded. The homer tube, sending out a constant-note signal, meant that a two-car team fitted with receiving apparatus could pinpoint the South African's every move.

Gradually, Sonders' route began to show more definite purpose. Bremse lifted the microphone, gave fresh instructions, then started the Volkswagen's engine.

'Your man has stopped not far from the garage where his second car waits,' he explained.

'Another homer tube?' queried Thane.

'But of course,' agreed his companion. 'And now we should soon know the true destination he intends.'

Sonders' fresh car was a Fiat, small, inconspicuous. He drove out of the garage, turned south along the short autobahn stretch of highway, then settled to a steady pace

111

along the narrow winding road skirting the shore of Lake Lucerne. Far behind, a young man on a motor scooter buzzed in the same direction. Behind him again, a small Renault van purred along, ready to take over the shadowing detail visually if necessary, its crew already tuned to the homer's note. Last in the procession, a mile to the rear, came the dusty Volkswagen driven by Kriminalinspektor Bremse.

The rain had dried out, clouds had dispersed, and Thane had his first opportunity to view the area tourist-style. The lake itself, broad and wide, had a distant fringe of mountains, many of them mistily snow-capped. As the road swung away from the lakeside, cutting through solid rock at points, reaching gradually into hilly farming country, Bremse gave a grunt.

'He is inconsiderate, this Sonders. There are other routes where you could see more of our mountains.'

His passenger had no complaints. The roadside was now speckled with picturesquely styled chalets, their shingled roofs high-peaked. The minute-sized fields, often set at dizzy angles on the hillsides, each had their quota of bell-clanging cattle. The scene might lack grandeur, but was oddly soothing.

The radio crackled again, and Bremse answered. When he replaced the microphone, his habitual cheerfulness had given way to grim satisfaction.

'He has turned off the road, and stopped,' he told Thane. 'Only a little way on, and then we must walk.'

Two minutes later the Volkswagen coasted to a standstill in a roadside clearing, already occupied by the motor scooter and the Renault van. Bremse got out, strode forward, and the nearest of the three waiting plain-clothes men saluted, then made his report. Royan Sonders' car had taken a left turn on to a narrow private road which led through trees to a chalet beyond . . . a big, rambling place with well-kept grounds and a double garage attached, reported Bremse's men.

'He is inside now,' said Bremse, lighting another of his

112

apparently inexhaustible supply of cigars. 'But one of my boys knows this place – it is, well, surprising.' He frowned. 'If your Sonders is a murderer, Herr Thane, what business does he have with a man of learning and culture?'

Thane felt a long-delayed tingle in his limbs. 'Who owns that house?'

'Professor Ernst Hundell.' Bremse puffed hard at his cigar until the tip glowed a satisfying cherry-red. 'Plenty of money – his family are bankers in Geneva. He is a major authority on Swiss history, which is an inspiring but complicated subject, my friend. Surprised?'

'Not completely.' The Scot gave a sigh of satisfaction. 'We've got plenty of time – maybe I should tell you what's been happening. Then you'll realize why it fits the pattern.' He began with Tinemann's death, sketched in the details up to and beyond Hollis's disappearance, and then his own gamble in following Sonders at a time when it might have been more reasonable to remain at the Scottish fishing village.

The Swiss inspector listened intently, interest increasing as the story unfolded. As Thane finished, he raised an expressive eyebrow. 'And now you think Sonders may have come here for what – advice?'

'Advice, encouragement, who knows?' Thane shrugged. 'He went to considerable trouble to try to shake any follower off his trail.'

'There is one way to find out,' mused Bremse. 'Herr Thane, once Sonders has gone on his way I think we should pay a visit of our own to Professor Hundell. Whatever happens, I will guarantee one thing – afterwards, Professor Hundell will find it extremely difficult to communicate with your Afrikaner.' His eyes twinkled. 'Sometimes these difficulties can last for a few days, even longer. Strange, isn't it?'

It was a long wait, but not unpleasant. The air was mild, Bremse's cigar-smoke acted as an effective midge repellant, and the van purred off at one stage to return with a supply of coffee, bread and cheese. Shortly after 9 p.m., as early dusk was spreading, one of the plain-clothes men scrambled back from his look-out post. Royan Sonders was leaving.

'The van can tail him,' decided Bremse. 'But his programme is obvious . . . back to Lucerne, change cars, then just sufficient time to drive to Basle and join the night plane to London. He will be met at London?'

'He'll be watched,' said Thane. 'Just sufficiently to make sure he heads straight back to the *Gabrielle*.'

'And to your building mousetrap,' murmured the Swiss policeman. 'Well, Herr Thane, perhaps we can yet produce a little additional cheese as bait, eh?'

Sidelights glowing in the deepening gloom, Royan Sonders' car went past their hiding place a minute later. As the red tail-lights began to fade in the distance, the police van growled off on its shadowing detail. Kriminalinspektor Bremse tossed away the stub of his cigar, ground it carefully under heel, and nodded towards his Volkswagen. They got in, he flicked the ignition key, and the little saloon began the short journey to the chalet.

'This Professor Hundell – does he speak English?' queried Thane. 'All right, I apologize; over here that's a dam' silly question.'

His companion gave a faint grin. 'Which you have answered yourself, my friend.'

The dust-covered police car purred to a halt outside the chalet's main door, the two policemen got out, walked across, then waited while Bremse's thudding blows on the antique brass knocker echoed in the air.

At last the door swung open. A middle-aged manservant gave them a querulous inspection, then changed his attitude at the sight of Bremse's warrant card. He ushered them in, asked them to wait in the broad hallway where the main decoration was a tall slim flower vase filled with a crown of brilliant blooms, and returned in a matter of seconds.

They followed him down the hallway, stopped while he opened the door opposite, were gestured into the room beyond, and then sensed the door close gently behind them. The room was snug and book-lined, a log fire burning bright in a large hearth of polished metal, an ancient cross-bow and broadsword hanging above its high mantelshelf.

'Good evening, gentlemen.' Professor Hundell, a tall stoop-shouldered man, white-haired and wearing thick horn-rim glasses, walked towards them leaning heavily on a stick. Thane placed him in his early sixties, recognized the drag in the historian's walk, and realized that the man had an artificial leg.

'Good evening, Herr Professor . . .' Inspector Bremse handled the introductions, and they shook hands, Professor Hundell's grasp firm and strong.

'Sit down, gentlemen.' He led them over to the fire, waited until each had settled, and then lowered himself into a high-backed leather armchair. 'When Julius – my servant – told me there were two police officers here, one from England, my first obvious reaction was curiosity. I take it there is a definite reason for the call?' He glanced at Bremse. 'You do not object if we speak in English, to aid your guest?'

The Swiss policeman nodded. 'Our visit is on Herr Thane's business, Professor. And' – he cleared his throat apologetically –'I must emphasize that as far as the Swiss police are concerned, we are extending co-operation. I would be happier to sit back by your fire, and leave Herr Thane to explain his purpose.'

'Hmm.' Professor Hundell frowned. 'In other words, this is connected with some matter in England.'

'Scotland, Professor Hundell,' corrected Thane. 'Scotland, and a visitor who has just left you, Royan Sonders.'

The historian gave a bleak smile. 'That much I had already managed to deduce, Chief Inspector Thane. But if this is not a matter for the Swiss police, what happens if I simply tell you that Herr Sonders is a friend, that he came here on a private visit, and that I decline to discuss the matter further?' The same coldly polite smile switched on once more. He sat back, picked up a straight-stemmed briar pipe from the low table beside his chair, and began filling the bowl from a brass tobacco-jar.

'In that case, there wouldn't be much I could do about it.' Quiet, deliberate emphasis sent Thane's words stabbing across the room. 'I would go back to a place called Sanctuary Isle, Professor, to try to find out on my own the connection between the murder of two good men and – and the Spanish Armada.'

One thumb-tip deep in the pipe bowl, Professor Hundell froze where he sat. Slowly, carefully, he placed the pipe on the table, then, an unspoken question on his lips, looked towards Bremse. The Swiss policeman nodded. 'It is as my friend says, Professor.'

'Murder – two murders?' The historian pursed his lips. 'But why come to see me, why suspect Herr Sonders?'

'For the same reason that I mentioned the Armada and you avoided it,' pressed Thane. 'You are an expert, Professor Hundell. Royan Sonders is a man who may be involved in two killings, killings which have some association with the Armada. When a man like Sonders visits an expert, I regard it as a consultation on a problem. What kind of problem do you bring to an historian? Surely only the type where the answer may have been obscured by the centuries!'

'I said he was a friend,' objected the Professor.

From the other chair, Kriminalinspektor Bremse gave a grunt. 'With respect, Herr Professor, do all your friends spend half an afternoon ducking and dodging through Lucerne and making secret changes of cars before they come to see you?'

'Professor' – Thane fired a salvo of his own. 'Who paid for the purchase of the yacht *Gabrielle*? Was it Sonders, or did he have a backer – maybe you?'

The historian's lips twisted bitterly. 'It might be easier, Herr Thane, much easier for us all, if I knew why you believe there may be a link between these murders and the

116

Armada – then let me judge for myself. Afterwards, my position might be different.'

'All right. First, accept that two men have died. Then, we found this scrap of burned paper. . . .' Thane sketched the web-like story of death and mystery which seemed to have its centre on the island bird sanctuary. Professor Hundell registered polite interest at first, but a frown creased his forehead as the story progressed, and by the time it ended his attitude was one of grim concern.

'What you have told me, Herr Thane, I did not know before – I had not even heard hinted at. But you admit you do not have proof to arrest either Royan Sonders or this man Preston?'

'I don't have the proof,' agreed Thane. 'But I may get closer to it if you tell me what you know, Professor.'

'Herr Professor' – Inspector Bremse began to speak, but the tall man opposite them cut him short.

'No need for warnings, Herr Bremse. I am aware of my situation.' The historian rose clumsily to his feet, gripped the stick, moved over to the hearth and stood staring into the flames. 'Chief Inspector, how much do you know about those ships of the Spanish Armada which reached Scotland?'

'Mainly that nearly all were wrecked and that only a few survivors reached shore. Both Scotland and Ireland have families who are still called "dark Spaniards" – probably descendants from intermarriage.'

'True.' Professor Hundell warmed to his subject as if the two detectives were one of his student classes. 'In particular, at least three Armada ships are known to have come to grief in the seas around the island of Mull. One was what you call the Tobermory galleon, the other two, according to the records, were wrecked near places called Salen and Lochaline. That these ships existed is fact. Their identities' – he gave a wry grimace – 'that is another matter. There have been arguments and counter-arguments, and the composition of this Armada did nothing to help. We know of eleven ships in that fleet which all bore the

117

name *Nuestra Senora*, eight called *San Juan* and the same number called *La Conception*!

'It was a bitter time, Herr Thane. Ships smashed to pieces in a hurricane gale, seamen struggling ashore to – if you will forgive me – a foreign land where the inhabitants often had a savage disregard for human life. Some lived, as you say. Others died. One ship was wrecked at a place called Fair Isle, which name I am told could be some sort of a joke. A few of its crew survived and took a year to make their way back to Spain.

'But that is incidental; we are interested only in two ships. The first is your Tobermory galleon, the one they call the treasure galleon, the payship. There are accounts which name it the *Florida*, the *Almirante de Florencia* and other versions. There are equally authentic records which say it was none of these, was not a treasure ship at all, but was a Sicilian vessel which sailed with the Armada, the *San Juan Bautista* . . . which, Herr Thane, was a fighting vessel and no treasure galleon.'

Thane gave a brief nod. So far, Hundell had told him nothing new. The smashed, wrecked Armada had left a legacy of confusion over the exact location of its coastal graveyards. Even at Tobermory, the latest series of salvage attempts, carried out in the 1950s, had yielded only a few trifles. Added alongside earlier meagre recoveries of coin, some plate and weapons, they only amounted to proof that an Armada ship lay deep under the off-shore silt.

Hundell turned from the hearth and gave a sigh. 'You ask, probably, why should this concern a student of Swiss history? Chief Inspector, about eighteen months ago I commenced a project, a new thesis on what we term the Golden League – a grouping of cantons in Switzerland formed just two years before the Armada sailed. These were years of religious differences, of what one might term mutual defence pacts. Some Swiss mercenary soldiers returned from France a few years after the league was founded, and played an important part as individuals in the . . . ah . . . manoeuvres which followed.

118

'Chief Inspector, I discovered some Spanish names among their numbers. The possibilities were intriguing, and I did still more research. But these Spaniards were not, as I had at first supposed, mere agents of their country. They were a small band – four, no more – of seamen who had been with the Armada and who had reached Switzerland via France. To me, this was an exciting little mystery – a mystery I managed to solve.'

Thane stirred with interest as the older man limped over to the desk in one corner of the room, jerked open a drawer, and extracted a thin file of stapled papers.

'This, Chief Inspector, is a typewritten transcript of a document I located in the archives of a village church in the canton of Obwalden – a canton where much of our early history was enacted. It is an account of the wanderings of one Juan Diego Vega, who was a petty officer or the equivalent aboard the galleon *Nuestra Senora del Santa Cruz*, a ship of a mere sixteen guns, small by comparison with the largest vessels of forty guns and more.

'But Vega's story makes her of vital interest. He claims that after the Spanish fleet was broken by the English the *Nuestra Senora* came alongside one of the fleet flagships, the *San Salvador*, which was crippled and helpless. What he describes as "six stout chests" were transferred aboard the *Nuestra Senora*, and the crew were charged to guard these chests come what may.'

'And the *Nuestra Senora*?' Thane knew what the reply must be.

'Is described by him as being wrecked on a reef of half-tide rocks which he places as being just south of the island of Mull. To use his own words as I translated them, "We who survived fulfilled our charge and reached the blessed isle of sanctuary, by which name all called it henceforth." Your Sanctuary Isle, Chief Inspector.'

'And the six chests?' Inspector Bremse, a fascinated spectator, prompted his countryman.

'Contained, without doubt, much of the true treasure of the Armada – gold and plate, specie, jewels of Orders of

Chivalry to be presented to the leaders of a victorious invasion. There was also, gentlemen, a crown, gem-studded, which history declares was given by the Vatican to be known as the new State Crown of England . . . a crown which has never been traced.'

'Sonders knew all this?' Almost automatically, Thane lit a cigarette then let it smoulder between his fingers.

'Yes. I needed help.' Professor Hundell looked away from him in obvious embarrassment. 'First, I made further research, and found that the records of the time showed that there was a belief that a fourth galleon had been lost in the Firth of Lorne – but there was no evidence as to its identity.

'Soon afterwards, I met Royan Sonders, a man who, by his talk, knew the sea . . . in this country, Chief Inspector, we are completely land-locked and such opportunities are not common. We had mutual friends – my family have considerable interests in finance – and Sonders was described to me as a man who was adventurous, prepared to gamble.'

'Professor, what you're trying to say is that you cooked up a deal with Sonders that he should go and try to locate the *Nuestra Senora's* treasure.' Thane stared at the historian in open bewilderment. 'Why? Why send him sneaking over as a faked-up playboy yachtsman? Why not go your-self, in an open, scientifically organized expedition?'

The man opposite suddenly appeared older, more stoop-shouldered. He flushed, stumbled for words. 'It was – no, you are right, Herr Thane. It would be only part excuse to say it was his idea. I told him what I knew because already I wondered if the treasure could be found. Can you under-stand, Herr Thane, I am not interested in this for personal reward? Kriminalinspektor Bremse will agree, my family has no lack of funds and I am a man who requires little. But I – yes, I fevered for this treasure, for what it repre-sented.' He gave a wry smile. 'It has been a madness perhaps, a delirium – with shock as the cure.'

Thane swore softly and efficiently. 'Why the hell – Professor, why couldn't you do it openly? Surely the credit –?'

'Credit I would have had, yes. The treasure? That is a very different matter.' Professor Hundell sat down wearily. 'The treasure of your Tobermory galleon belongs to your Duke of Argyll. For three hundred years the wreck has been the property of his family by gift of Royal charter. Only the crown, if recovered, becomes the property of the State. But if the Tobermory treasure is not there, but at Sanctuary Isle, what legal situation arises? Again, if the Duke has no claim, then your strange laws of treasure trove apply. There have been recent cases, archaeological discoveries which the State has declared its own. But your Scottish law declares that concealment is not a criminal offence. The offence is when, the discovery known, the finder refuses to surrender the results of his labours.'

'So your plan was concealment – to have your own secret treasure-house.' Thane growled the words, but still felt a human understanding of the historian's motives. 'What was Sonders' rake-off? How much would he get?'

'The remainder after I had chosen those items of historical interest which I wished to retain.'

Thane winced. 'Two murders probably rate as minor overheads to Sonders right now. Why did he come here tonight?'

'To report progress,' shrugged Professor Hundell. 'He merely said that it had been slow, that there were difficulties. He sought a fresh guidance from the account of Juan Diego Vega.'

'That means . . .' Thane paused as a new realization sank home. 'Professor, do you know exactly where these six chests are hidden?'

The Swiss historian shook his head. 'No. Vega's account amounted to an enigma. He said that they placed their charge "in the keeping of both land and water, where grey sentinels keep watch beside a place of rest." At first we thought this must mean an area to the north of the Isle, where there is a breeding ground for seals. Now, Sonders says he is convinced that the answer is simpler – an old abandoned well on the island.'

'I know the place,' agreed Thane. 'It's overlooked by a ridge of grey rock – and there's what might be called a place of rest, a trace of the ruins of what must have been a building at one time.' He glanced at Bremse, and the two policemen rose. 'Professor, I'm not fool enough to even guess at the extent of action which may have to be taken. I can make absolutely no promise in return, but I'm asking you not to make any attempt to contact Sonders.'

'It would be unwise as well as unfriendly,' murmured Kriminalinspektor Bremse. 'It would also be difficult.'

'I understand.' The historian struggled to his feet and, using his stick, limped with them towards the door. 'Herr Thane, sorrow mends little, but you have my pledge as far as Royan Sonders is concerned.'

They went out into the hallway, past the tall slim vase with its bouquet of long-stemmed yellow flowers, each individual stem rich in petals. Thane glanced at them again, and Professor Hundell smiled weakly.

'They are pleasant, are they not? They are one of my garden favourites, yet here they also grow wild on the mountain slopes.'

'Handsome to look at,' agreed Thane. 'What are they?'

'Wolfsbane is our name for the plant, though in Britain I think you call it monkshood.' Professor Hundell leaned on his stick as he added, 'The catalogue name, of course, is Aconitum lycoctonum.'

Chief Detective Inspector Thane reacted as if stung. 'Aconite?'

'Of that genus,' nodded the historian. 'They are a hardy perennial. Perhaps you would like a cutting to take back with you? Of course, a little care is required in handling the root, its juice can be poisonous . . .' His voice trailed away as he realized both detectives were staring at the flowers, grim fascination on their faces. 'Chief Inspector –' he swallowed. 'You did not tell me how these two men died.'

'One by aconite poisoning,' said Thane, recovering from the initial surprise. 'Professor, did you –'

'Yes.' The Swiss half-shut his eyes, swayed, then steadied himself. 'My apologies, gentlemen. I feel just a little unwell. On Royan Sonders' last visit he asked me for some roots of wolfsbane. He said he wanted them for a friend who had a garden. I gave him several roots.'

'How long ago?'

'That would be less than two weeks back, on his last visit.' The older man swayed again. 'Now I must rest for a little. Good night, gentlemen.'


It was early afternoon the following day before Thane reached Inverlay, the dull ache in the vicinity of his temples a reminder of Kriminalinspektor Bremse's enthusiastic hospitality, a new cautious respect for native Swiss brandy as one educational dividend from the experience.

After the second leg of the air journey had brought him to Glasgow, there had been a long interview with Chief Superintendent Ilford, a time for waiting while the C.I.D. boss conferred with the Chief Constable who, in turn, contacted his Argyll counterpart, and, finally, agreement. He travelled north by police car knowing that, while he could expect no official backing if his plan came unstuck, everyone would be very happy if it succeeded.

'Heads they win, tails you lose,' grunted Phil Moss in a cynical snarl at the ways of authority.

'It'll work out,' declared Thane with hopeful optimism. 'Incidentally, what's happened to the press brigade? I thought they'd be hanging around in droves.'

His second-in-command gave a snort. 'We're no longer news, Colin. They've gone charging over to Edinburgh on a "triangle" killing . . . beautiful model and rich boy friend, then boy friend's wife turns up with a gun. Worth more in circulation figures than a bird sanctuary killing.'

'Conveniently for us,' mused Thane. He turned to practicalities: 'Buddha Ilford said MacMaster's post mortem report on Hollis was complete. Have you seen it?'

'Huh-huh, and it's hardly inspiring,' grunted Moss. 'Main cause of death was a blow from a blunt instrument which crushed the skull. Hollis was as good as dead – even before he went into the water.' He slid the typewritten p.m. summary across the table.

In his usual bald prose, Professor MacMaster reported that lungs and stomach showed Hollis had probably lived for a few seconds after entering the water, but not long enough to drown. Time of death, however, he regarded as a tricky subject. His verdict was based on two factors, 'Rigor mortis, originally present, was beginning to fade. This, in conjunction with certain temperature tests . . .'

Thane put down the report and shook his head. 'I've been reading 'em for years, Phil, but these clinical reports still give me the shivers. Well, he says death occurred 34 to 38 hours before examination – as far as we're concerned, that's any time in the four hours immediately after Hollis was seen on the quayside on his way to make a second call on Finn Preston's boat. And if he landed in the water almost immediately after his skull was smashed, then the attack was either on a boat or at the water's edge.'

'Cigarette?' Moss extended his packet, they shared a match, and then Thane turned to the rest of the report summaries which had gathered.

Some, at least gave cause for satisfaction. Phil Moss's contact with the London bookshop had confirmed his hunch that Captain Tinemann had been sent two volumes on Elizabethan history, both particular authorities on the Spanish Armada.

The next was even more important. The sacking-wrapped section of wood they'd found in the bird warden's store-shed, brought ashore and sent south by car for examination, had been positively identified as African oak, 'age uncertain, but positively of considerable antiquity.' African oak – the main building material used in many of the old Spanish sailing ships.

The police guard had been withdrawn from the Isle, and Inspector Davidson's formal notification that this had 'proved necessary because of manpower shortage' gave no indication of the fact that the move had been inspired by Thane – the Argyll County officer was living up to his determination to carry his own share of any repercussions that might lie in the future.

The final item was a fresh piece of confirmation of the situation. The obscure mathematical calculation found beside the Armada dates on the flame-seared paper had at last made sense – as a simple exercise which had as its basis the current value of gold per ounce. Captain Tinemann seemed to have passed an idle hour or so finding the value of the yellow metal in multiples of a pound weight!

Detective Inspector Moss shuffled the report sheets into a neat bundle. 'There's still a blank, Colin. How did Tinemann latch on to the treasure in the first place? One piece of timber wouldn't be enough.'

'That's true and I think he originally took on the job of bird warden in all innocence,' agreed the burly C.I.D. chief. 'There had to be some positive indication, Phil – and remember, he'd started to clean out that old well. Whatever he found, it's probably on Finn Preston's boat at this moment.'

'Ach, all this probability business is bad for the nerves,' complained Moss. He sniffed in mock derision. 'With due respect to your superior rank, I'm not looking forward to going back into uniform and pounding a beat. If this stunt of yours doesn't flush things out into the open . . .'

'It should, Phil,' said Thane soberly. 'I've checked and double-checked. There was a *San Salvador* in the Armada – with the Spanish paymaster-general aboard. It was damaged, and its treasure was off-loaded – there's plenty of authority to back up the facts.'

'And the stuff's lying out there, instead of at Tobermory!' Phil Moss admitted a slight sense of awe. 'Once the news gets out –'

'This place will be invaded by every foot-loose tourist in Christendom,' growled Thane. 'Half of them with buckets and spades in case there's a gold bar or two still lying around.'

He got up, went over to the cell's small, high-set window and, standing on tip-toe, peered out through its bars. The blue waters of the Firth of Lorne were peaceful, bathed in sunshine, here and there embroidered by the white of wave-crests. Close to the horizon line, Sanctuary Isle appeared as a faint grey blob, the tower of its automatic light visible and no more.

'Our bait's out there, Phil – probably at the bottom of the old well. The kind of bait that adds up to an overpowering temptation. It's been waiting there for almost four hundred years, ever since these poor devils of Spaniards hid it away. Now it's going to help spring our trap – and whoever we catch, he's going to give us enough of the truth to break this case.' He turned away from the window and came back to the table. 'Let's get down to details. Willie MacPherson knows the drill?'

Moss nodded. 'He's ready and willing – and he's got a boat hidden. Colin, do you really believe there's thirty million quid hidden on the Isle?'

'No. That's the Tobermory legend – the historians say the figure's been inflated over the years. There's probably only about ten million worth.'

'Only!'

'Aye, it would still buy a lot of groceries.' Thane grinned. 'Why worry? We won't get any of it – you'll just have to last out until we start drawing retirement pension.'

# Chapter Six

Chief Detective Inspector Colin Thane's plan was relatively simple, its main elements a smoke-screen of police activity to suggest that interest had turned away from Sanctuary Isle, and the fact that though Willie MacPherson's launch was openly moored at its customary berth in Inverlay harbour the boatman had a second, smaller vessel lying hidden and ready only a mile along the shore. By 4 p.m. Thane had settled the last details of the night's operation and, leaving Phil Moss to make final arrangements, left the police station and walked down to the harbour.

There was a small crowd of about a score of fishermen, villagers and a fringe of school-children gathered by the harbour breakwater, all gazing seawards. Joining them, he saw the cause of their interest. Less than a mile off shore, three huge black shapes gambolled on the surface, now diving, now lunging from the waves to expose the length of their smooth sleek forms, smacking down again in a creaming of foam.

'Basking sharks, Chief Inspector, big 'uns. You don't get a sight like that near the city, eh?'

He turned, and recognized the chunkily-built fisherman by his side, Skipper Gault of the *Lenore Glen*. 'They're big enough brutes,' agreed Thane. 'Do you often get them as close inshore?'

The fisherman nodded. 'It happens about this time of the year. These 'uns are in a playful mood – and there's plenty more further out in the Firth.' He chuckled. 'There's the

127

*Rock Rose* on her way out – I wondered when Preston'd get moving!'

Engine growling, the red-hulled motor sailer emerged from the harbour mouth, bobbing afresh as it met open sea, and then began a ruler-straight course towards the spot where the basking sharks continued to plunge. Finn Preston was on deck, his wife at the wheel, and the bronze-bearded Viking moved at top speed as he stripped the canvas cover from the *Rock Rose's* single for'ard mounted harpoon gun.

'That's a two-pounder he's got there,' grunted Skipper Gault. 'Fires a double-barbed harpoon, line attached – and he's ruddy well welcome to it. A basker's quiet enough, in fact it gets its name from the way it usually floats almost on the surface in calm weather, its back just above the water as if it was enjoying the sunshine. But give it a fright, or stick one of these harpoons in it, and you've got trouble.'

Fascinated, Thane watched as the little motor sailer closed the distance on the three sharks, each of which was almost its equal in length.

'Preston knows his business,' murmured the fisherman by his side. 'He's getting up-wind of them – pity you don't have binoculars, Chief Inspector, there's a crafty bit of work involved. He'll cut his engine any minute and hoist sail. Preston swears the propeller vibrations scare 'em off – look now!'

The *Rock Rose*, now diminished to toy-like proportions, suddenly blossomed an expanse of red canvas mainsail which filled in the wind.

Ninety, sixty, now forty yards separated the motor sailer from the nearest of its plunging prey.

'They aim just behind the gills,' said Skipper Gault – and as he spoke, a dull bark came across the water. Instantly, one of the three basking sharks disappeared, then emerged again, leaping high from the water, hitting the surface in a white cloud of spray, diving again. Its two companions had disappeared, sliding down into the depths.

Around them, the crowd began to disperse. 'The rest is time and luck,' said Skipper Gault. 'There he goes . . .' The *Rock Rose*, which had slowed in the water, was moving, gaining pace, its sail hanging limp. 'The fish is towing him. Maybe for an hour, maybe a lot more. Depends on whether he gets a chance of another clean shot at it . . . or on whether the shark's rogue enough to turn.'

Thane nodded. The battle out there had only begun, man versus thirty feet of barrel-shaped fast-diving small-brained bone and muscle, strong as a railway engine.

'What happens once Preston nails it?' he asked.

The fisherman shrugged. 'Depends on whereabouts the thing takes him. Sometimes he tows the whole carcase, other times he butchers it and lets the main carcase sink – he's got to deliver to an off-shore depot up near Oban.'

Either way, mused Thane, Finn Preston was going to be kept busy for the next few hours. And that well suited his own plans.

As the last of the crowd left to return to everyday matters, Thane continued his walk along the quayside. Then he stopped and grinned as he saw the little all-white speedboat which was purring its way into the harbour. Fate was apparently still playing on his side – he'd been contemplating a visit to the *Gabrielle*, and now the yacht's owner was saving him the trouble. Royan Sonders swept the speedboat round in a final tight-ruddered curve, cut the twin outboard motors, and let the boat's momentum carry it the last few feet to the quayside. He tied a bow-rope to an iron rung projecting from the quay wall, then scrambled ashore as Thane strode towards him.

'Hello, Mr Sonders – I'd heard you'd got back. Good trip?' Thane's tone was cheerfully hearty.

The South African was momentarily surprised, then beamed his usual gold-toothed welcome. 'The usual sort of journey,' he agreed. 'There and back as quickly as I could get it over with. I'd some business in Lucerne – tiresome but necessary.' He stepped nearer, his face more serious, his manner confidential. 'I heard about Edgar Hollis's

129

body being found, Chief Inspector – my crew told me almost as soon as I got back this morning. Was it . . .?'

'Murder?' Thane gave a solemn nod. 'Keep it to yourself, Mr Sonders, but there's little doubt about it. Or' – he glanced around with apparent caution – 'about who did it. You'll remember telling us you thought there was a fishing boat's crew on the quayside when you brought Hollis ashore from the *Gabrielle*? Well, we managed to locate them, and the last they saw of Mr Hollis, he was heading towards Finn Preston's boat!'

Royan Sonders' eyes glinted at the news, but his reaction was carefully controlled. 'Doesn't look too good for him, does it?' he said with a prim pursing of his mouth.

'It does not,' agreed Thane. 'We're just waiting until we get a few more threads in the weave, Mr Sonders. I want to tidy up both cases at once – and the proof I need isn't around here. Preston's had money trouble recently. I'm working on the line that he may have been borrowing from Captain Tinemann – and that when Mr Hollis said the Bird Society would run him straight into court if he went near the Isle that meant another blow financially. The seals out there represent cash to Preston and . . .' He stopped, smiled, and shook his head. 'I'm talking too much, Mr Sonders. And you could be an important witness at the end of the day. Anyway, it's time I was moving. Inspector Moss and I will be spending most of our time at Oban tonight and probably tomorrow as well. We're trying to make quite sure about Preston's financial background. Forty-eight hours, Mr Sonders – then he won't be catching any sharks for a long time.'

As a ham actor, Thane appeared to have scored a success. Royan Sonders made profuse promise that he'd keep the information to himself. They strolled back along the quayside together, stopped just short of the village main street, and parted – Sonders on his way to the post office, Thane heading for the Inverlay Arms with the expressed intention of checking out of his room and settling his bill.

Ten minutes later, the task completed, he left the little hotel and, overnight grip in one hand, strode along to the police station. He entered just as Phil Moss laid down the telephone.

'Well, the Post Office are co-operating as arranged,' said Moss. 'That was the exchange supervisor. They've just handled a telegram sent by Sonders. He has ordered five hundred gallons of oil fuel from a bunkering agent on the Clyde. Does that suggest anything?'

'That he feels confident he is pretty nearly ready to go home,' said Thane, laying down the grip. 'Got your supply of sea-sickness pills ready?'

Detective Inspector Moss gave a glum nod. 'Seriously, Colin, couldn't we have had the navy in on this deal?'

'We could, but we won't.' Thane was adamant. 'The Chief Constable made the same suggestion to Buddha Ilford – said he was pretty sure he only had to whisper "Armada treasure" to the Admiralty and he'd have a couple of motor gunboats placed at our disposal.' He shook his head. 'Let's face it, Phil, if the navy moved even a small unit into this coast the word would be spread by every fisherman in the Firth of Lorne. Half of these fishing boats have radio-telephone, and there's nothing a skipper likes better than a microphone gossip with his pals.'

His second-in-command resigned himself to the dangers ahead. 'It'll be chilly,' he muttered. 'Maybe I'd better wear an extra pullover.'

They left the village by car at 6 p.m., making a considerable ceremony of being seen off by Inspector Davidson. As the car drew away, Phil Moss was reasonably sure that he caught a glimpse of a familiar figure standing in a doorway across the street – Gino, Sonders' cook-steward. If he was right, the South African would very quickly have word of their departure. And Thane was taking no chances of their bluff being called. The police Jaguar travelled the hour's journey to Oban, they solemnly booked in at one of

131

the big hotels on the Highland holiday town's seafront, visited the police station, and then, with three hours still in hand, settled down in the warm comfort of the hotel lounge.

At 10 p.m., the first hint of dusk in the sky, the two detectives had a brief supper, then left the hotel by a rear door. An elderly saloon car, property of one of the Oban constables, was in the lane outside with its ignition key in the lock. They got in, Thane took the wheel, and the car, running with a slightly rheumatic clatter of engine tappets, drove quietly out of town and took the south road. Following the directions Moss read from his notebook, Thane stayed on the main highway for about fifteen miles, then took a right fork, the start of a long up-and down-hill haul over roads which became progressively narrower. Dusk was giving way to darkness, and they travelled on with headlights dipped, the sky overhead a deepening velvet. A thin and sickly moon, often blanketed by the heavy, lumbering cloud-shapes which drifted on the west wind, did little to detract from the pinhole glitter of stars which peeped through every cloud-gap.

'Slow here, Colin,' instructed Moss as another signpost loomed ahead. 'Aye, this is us – Lochan Reach. Turn right again, and pull in after about five hundred yards.'

Thane nodded, changed gear, and the car growled on. Five hundred yards, Willie MacPherson had said, and he was standing at that exact spot as the old car coasted to a halt.

'You are on time, Chief Inspector,' he complimented as the two men got out. 'Och, and it's a good thing, too.'

'The Fangs?' queried Thane. These waiting half-tide rocks and their fierce surrounding tidal race were beginning to play more and more on his imagination, a process encouraged by thoughts of the long-ago Spanish ship which had ripped on the sharp granite teeth, neither the first nor the last vessel and her crew to discover the terror which lay so close to Sanctuary Isle.

But the boatman shook his head. 'No, not this time, Mr

132

Thane. The tide reached high water mark about ten minutes ago, so we will have a nice quiet trip across. It's just that you're wanting to go over without being noticed – and though I wouldn't be knowing how long it will last, the cloud in the sky right now will make the water seem almost as black as the Earl of Hell's waistcoat, and himself all we need to meet out there to scare me right out of my skin.'

'Worried, Willie?' Phil Moss twinkled at the boatman's obvious unhappiness.

'Worried?' MacPherson was indignant. 'I am not worried, Inspector Moss. I am terrified. And there is a considerable difference, believe me.'

They left the road, scrambled over a low dry-stone dyke, swished their way through a bank of long, already dew-wet grass, and then reached the beach, a stretch of pebble-bouldered foreshore stretching twenty feet from the water's edge.

Willie MacPherson had hidden his boat with care, in the shadowed lee of a coffin-shaped mass of rock. The boat was an open twelve-footer, with a compact outboard motor clamped to the stern thwart, propeller arm canted at an angle to save it from contact until the vessel was back in the water.

'If you will both give a bit of a shove, then we'll be on our way,' he declared. 'It's no a bad wee boat at all – it belongs to my cousin Lachie. Mind you, I'd rather be taking out my own launch.'

'Maybe,' said Thane. 'But your launch is doing a valuable job of work right now, just lying unattended at Inverlay harbour. These are big fish we're after, Willie. Bigger and a dam' sight brainier than any of Finn Preston's basking sharks.'

They got together to heave the boat down to the water's edge. Soon its bow was chuckling through the wavelets, the outboard motor throttled back to a discreet whisper. As the coastline receded and the boatman steered a course towards the beacon-flash of Sanctuary Isle's automatic light, other lights glittered a little to the south. They had rounded a headland and, unseen and unheard, were running well clear of Inverlay harbour.

Feeling secure in terms of distance, the boatman opened the engine throttle a fraction and the whisper changed to a muffled, quickening burble before settling down to a steady throb. Thane edged near to him in the stern. 'Willie, when we get out to the Isle I want to make a landing at the north tip, by the seal rocks.'

In the darkness he could just make out the brief nod of acknowledgement – then suddenly MacPherson gave an oath, slammed the outboard's gear lever into reverse, and sat rigid, staring straight ahead. The boat slowed, wallowed, then moved steady sternwards, its engine maintaining the same quiet note.

'Hey, what's up?' demanded Phil Moss from the bow.

'There – dead ahead,' said the boatman softly. 'If we'd rammed that thing it wouldn't listen to apologies.'

The two city-bred policemen strained their eyes in the direction indicated. Then, as the moon's pallid glow filtered through a threadbare patch of cloud, they were hypnotized by the sight of the great black sail-like triangle sticking from the water little more than a couple of boat-lengths ahead. The basking shark was resting quietly, motionless, an eerie sight as the waves ebbed and flowed where the main bulk of its body began beneath the surface. As he watched, the huge fin, four feet in length, gave one slow rippling movement, then was still.

It seemed an age before Willie MacPherson was satisfied that they were sufficiently clear. Gently, carefully, he moved the outboard's gear lever to forward, slid the tiller bar to starboard, and steered in a wide arc round the resting monster.

'Man, man,' he muttered. 'I'm glad to be clear of that one.'

Phil Moss gulped and nodded agreement.

The boat crept the last half-mile to the Isle, engine at little more than tick-over. Thane was convinced that they'd arrived ahead of any other visitor and that Sonders, if he came out believing the Isle unguarded, would head directly to the landing place in the crescent bay or, failing that, would choose to come ashore on the west beach, the nearest point to the abandoned well with its lure of hidden treasure. . . . But 'take no chances' was still his guiding principle as far as this stage of the operation was concerned.

Quiet though the boat's approach might be, it still disturbed some of the Isle's inhabitants. A quick chorus of startled grunts, a score of soft splashes around them, showed that the seals in the vicinity were alarmed by this visitor nosing in out of the darkness and were taking avoiding action.

Deftly, MacPherson conned the boat through a minor maze of egg-shaped half-submerged boulders and beached his charge on the tiny half-moon of sandy shore beyond. He killed the engine, jumped over the side, splashed through the few inches of water, and had their craft bow-moored in a matter of moments.

'From up front, Chief Inspector,' he advised in a hoarse whisper. 'That way you'll keep your feet dry.'

They followed him on to the sand, and now Thane took the lead in a slow-moving Indian file progress, his goal one of the sheltering mounds of broken rock, rounded boulder and high-tufted vegetation, strategically positioned a scant fifty yards north of the well's site. Their feet scrunched over the sand and gravel, then they reached a stretch of rush-grass.

With a banshee screech a shape rose almost beneath Thane's feet. A brushing of feathered wings raked his face as a seabird, cawing indignation, spurted skywards to avoid being trampled. Another followed, and from several points nearby came the sound of other birds girning, stirring and then, as the three men waited, gradually settling.

Thane's heart steadied from its momentary mad tattoo to a more regular rhythm, he moved one hand in a 'forward' signal, and, cautiously, they crossed the remaining distance.

'And now, Mr Thane?' asked MacPherson as they settled into a natural hollow in the rocks.

'No smoking, no talking,' said Thane softly. 'Just watch and wait.'

They did, for two cramped, shivering hours while the rock surface around lost the last remnant of its day-time warmth and became almost icy to the touch. Thane weakened sufficiently to allow both himself and Phil Moss one well-shielded cigarette. Willie MacPherson refused a similar puff, but instead offered sips from a flat pint-sized metal flask of 'triple-run' he produced from the depths of an inside pocket. Every thirty seconds there was a momentary flash of brilliance over to their left as the Isle beacon swept its signal.

Five minutes before 2 a.m. they heard the steady growl of an approaching motor boat, travelling at half-throttle.

'No navigation lights,' growled MacPherson, shifting into a more comfortable position.

The beacon swept, and Thane caught a fragmentary impression of a black shape crossing the flickering shimmer of water. Whoever was in the boat was in no hurry. It made a throbbing patrol round the crescent bay, turned north, its engine note fading a little and finally, after making an east to west half-circle round the Isle, retraced its course.

'Going in for the landing place now,' breathed MacPherson.

Thane nodded. 'What do you make of it, Willie? Recognize the engine?'

The man shook his head. 'It's nothing big, Mr Thane . . . but it's not Sonders' wee speedboat either.'

'He's got another boat slung aboard the *Gabrielle*,' volunteered Phil Moss. 'A fourteen footer, I'd say – and it's got an engine.'

'That could be it,' agreed MacPherson. 'We'll find out soon enough – he's throttling back, coming in to land.'

The engine died, and this time the seabird alarm system operated in the favour of the hidden trio. The silence was broken first by the faintest scuffing of feet on rock and then by the shriek of an outraged gull. A voice swore, other gulls rose in a flapping, calling circle, black shapes in the almost equally black sky where the faint, sickly moon was now swathed in cotton-wool cloud, casting only a faint glow over the island.

'Colin . . .' Phil Moss dug his sharp, bony elbow into the Millside C.I.D. chief's side and pointed towards the well site. 'Got them,' whispered Thane.

He counted the vague figures appearing that short stone's throw away, sensing as much as seeing them. One – two – three men altogether. Three – Sonders had a crew of four on the *Gabrielle*. It seemed certain that Sonders would have taken the basic precaution of leaving one man on guard aboard the yacht – and perhaps another on guard beside the launch which had brought them out to Sanctuary Isle.

For the first time, carefully dimmed and shaded hand-torches suddenly flickered. Two of the men below were carrying an assortment of equipment, and one of them, laying down the bulk of his load, was now adjusting what looked like a broom with a frying-pan on one end. He put on headphones, and Thane gave a taut smile of appreciation. Government surplus mine detectors – handy little items which would locate most forms of buried metal. There was even a vet in England somewhere who used them to check whether animals in his area had swallowed iron nails or similar scrap.

The man with the mine detector began moving it slowly over the surface, walking in a regular, snail-like pattern while the detector swung its slow and constant survey.

Jab – the same elbow dug again into Thane's ribs, and he glared a wincing protest at his second-in-command. Phil Moss held up three fingers of one hand, three of the other, and the quick mime which followed had only one interpretation – 'do we jump 'em?'

He made up his mind that the answer was yes, but waved a sudden negative as a new development occurred among the treasure-seeking trio. The mine detector operator gave a hoarse cry, ripped the headphones from his ears, and offered them to one of his companions. The second man listened at the same spot, gave the first a hearty slap on the back, then passed the equipment to their companion.

Two short, sharp whistle-blasts shrilled at that instant – and Thane, his own police whistle already in his hand, spun round in surprise. The whistle signal came again, from the direction of the seal rocks where Willie Mac-Pherson had brought their boat ashore!

The signal's effect on the treasure-hunters was equally electrifying. Moving with swift efficiency, they scooped up their equipment and began running towards the landing place and their own boat. Feet pattered and grated on the rock, their shapes seemed to melt into the depths of the formless night.

In the hollow, Thane scrambled to his feet, the others following his example.

'Let's get after 'em,' urged Phil Moss.

'But our boat, Chief Inspector' – Willie MacPherson tugged at his elbow in anxiety. 'They must have found our boat! And they'll be out on the water in their own craft any minute!'

In confirmation, the other boat's engine growled to life moments later, climbing through the revs with no attempt at muffling or concealment.

'We'll head back,' snapped Thane. 'Sonders has to make his way back to the *Gabrielle*, now or later – we'll catch up with him. Hell, I thought that if there was a man missing, they'd left him guarding their own launch. Come on . . .'

They set off at a scrambling run, crashing through the low scrub grass, tripping, swearing, almost falling as they crossed the barren waste of shingle and boulder beyond. Jumping and clawing over the last line of boulders, they came to a sudden stop while Thane played his torch-beam on the stretch of sand below.

The boat was still there, its mooring rope intact. Two strange flipper-like marks on the sand beside it told their own story.

'A ruddy frogman,' cursed Moss. 'No wonder he got round behind us.'

They got down beside the boat, MacPherson climbed aboard, snapped on his own torch and made a hurried check.

'Everything okay?' queried Thane.

'Seems so,' agreed the boatman. 'Listen, sir – that launch – it's coming this way.'

'Picking up the frogman, then getting out fast,' growled Thane. 'Start her up, Willie – let's see if we can beat them to it.'

The boatman nodded. The two detectives untied the mooring line, tossed it aboard, then, as they thrust the lightweight craft's bow clear of the sand into the water and scrambled aboard, soaking shoes, socks and trouser legs in the process, MacPherson yanked the outboard's starter-line and the engine fired in healthy vigour. Stern-first the twelve-footer threaded its way through the broken neck-lace of sea-washed rock, swung, then, as the boatman engaged forward drive and the propeller blades bit the water, it arrowed out into the Firth, white phosphorescence boiling from its quickening wake. MacPherson was steering by ear, on a straight course towards the sound of the other craft. They heard the heavier note of its engine slow as if idling, then resume its full-throated beat.

'He's aboard' – Phil Moss didn't finish. Their own engine-note changed. The beat became a splutter, a strangled cough, and finally died altogether.

'Hell damn the thing!' Willie MacPherson pulled the choke lever, yanked the starter cord and swore, pulled, yanked and swore again, and finally gave a groan. 'I haff the most horrible notion, Chief Inspector. Hold your torch steady here a moment. . . .'

Thane obeyed, watching while the boatman unscrewed the filler cap on the fuel tank, dipped one long forefinger into the tank, drew it out, and tasted the result.

'The black-hearted' – his voice was despairing. 'Och, he left the boat alone, I thought. The treacherous –'

Thane growled him short. 'What's up?'

'Water, salt water poured in with the petrol,' said Mac-Pherson, grim concern entering his words. 'There would be enough clean fuel in the carburetter and fuel line to bring us out here – but the rest is useless.'

The other boat growled closer, a moving blob of black on the moon-greyed sea. A sardonic hail rang across the water.

'Having trouble?' Sorry we can't stop, Preston – but you would meddle!' The words ended in a roar of laughter, and the engine noise began to fade as the boat turned away.

'What the hell did he mean, "Preston"?' snapped Moss. 'Look, how long will it take us to get this thing moving again?'

'Preston's motor sailer carries a dinghy like this one,' said Thane quietly, still holding the torch steady. 'They must think this is his boat.'

'Aye, and they've fixed us good and proper.' MacPherson screwed the filler cap back on the fuel tank in slow, mechanical fashion. 'There's nothing I can do about it, Mr Thane – even if I cleaned out the whole fuel system, there's no spare petrol aboard.' He sighed. 'Not even a distress flare, either – and we'll be needing them soon. Take a look towards the Isle, a steady look, and you'll see what I mean.'

The carefully restrained undertone of tension in his voice made them obey without question. The low-lying mass of Sanctuary Isle, its beacon light flashing, seemed unchanged, and yet there was something different, something happening as they watched.

'We – we're drifting south, and pretty fast.' Realization

seared home to Thane. 'Willie, what's the state of the tide?'

'It's on the way out, well on the turn. Low tide should be in about another couple of hours, Chief Inspector. Ach, if we had the engine it wouldn't be a worry – there would still be time to be getting clear of the south race. But' – he shrugged significantly – 'we're being pulled out on the ebb, out into the run of the tidal race. It's no' a very nice situation, I'm afraid, and us with not even an oar aboard – thanks to my cousin Lachie, who is too dam' mean to be doing anything properly at all.'

A greedy, ten-knot current hungry to sweep their tiny craft down towards the shoal reef with its wave-dashed run of savage, broken water and the jagged, waiting rocks of the half-tide Fangs. . . . Thane felt his stomach tighten.

'We could tear out these centre-thwart boards, and use them as paddles,' suggested Phil Moss. 'Maybe get ourselves back on to the Isle.'

'It wouldn't be worth the try.' The boatman shook his head. 'Not now.'

The boat, silent except for an occasional creak of a timber, the lap of a wave against its side, was moving further away from the Isle with every passing second. Those wave-laps were increasing in frequency and, slowly, almost imperceptibly, in strength. A south-west wind and a north-east tidal race formed a combination which was combing the surface of the water to unruly life.

'Damn it, let's try paddling,' protested Moss, his voice thin and irate. 'What have we got to lose?'

Together, they wrenched the two wooden struts of the thwart clear of their mountings. As paddles, the struts were thick and clumsy – but it was that or bare hands.

Thane on one side, Moss on the other, they got to work while Willie MacPherson stayed by the stern, his torch now flashing hopeful dots and dashes towards the distant mainland. Slowly, the two detectives managed to turn the dinghy's bow towards the Isle again – but turning was one thing, making progress across the pull of the current another.

They were clear of the immediate shelter of the bird sanctuary's mass – and first notice was served by a drenching cloud of spray as a rolling, white-crested wavetop, larger than its fellows, broke along the little craft's port quarter. The moonlight strengthened with ironic timing, giving a view of black-green rollers, phosphorescent tipped, meeting and merging, creaming and blending, only a little way beyond.

'Get her bow into them!' MacPherson's plea was urgent. The two detectives sweated at their primitive paddles, abandoning their original goal. The bow crept round again – and then the dinghy vibrated with new life, floundering and pitching as the full ten-knot race clutched her hull and began pulling her along.

'Well, gentlemen, that is it settled.' The boatman gave a wry grimace, fumbled in his pocket and took out his flask. 'Perhaps you would care to be joining me in a last sip – to leave good liquor to go spoiled would be a sinful waste.'

Phil Moss shook his head, tried to light a cigarette, and swore savagely as a white curtain of spray soaked tobacco and extinguished match.

'Chief Inspector?' The Highlander's courtesy was strained but unbroken. 'A sip, and my apologies with it.'

Thane took the flask, raised it to his lips while the dinghy tossed anew, then lowered the flask again and clapped the palm of his hand over the opened lip of the container.

If it would work, if his memory was true. . . . 'Willie, this liquor is the same stuff I tasted at your mother's place, isn't it?'

'And good triple-run spirit at that,' agreed MacPherson. 'Though we may not have too long to enjoy it. You see thon line of white about a mile ahead, Chief Inspector? That's a welcome from The Fangs.' He grabbed the gunwale of the boat as it slumped into the rolling canyon formed by the meeting of two waves, then tossed a drenched path over their peak.

'If this liquor is as good as the other stuff, it'll turn the engine,' declared Thane. 'We can try it, man. Any tools aboard?'

'Aye, a few,' confirmed the boatman cautiously. 'But –'

'Don't ruddy well argue,' snarled Thane, moving crab-like towards the stern. 'Phil – Phil, come and hold the torch. Willie, you're going to disconnect the fuel feedpipe to the carburetter. Hurry, man. Then get the top off the carburetter and clean out the bowl – but for God's sake don't let any of this damned spray get in.'

The Highlander's startled glance showed his belief that Thane had cracked under the strain.

'Get on with it,' urged Thane. 'I'm not crazy – it'll work. Alcohol's a fuel, isn't it? This flask is alcohol, more or less – probably more!'

At last the other man understood. His hands moved with clumsy speed, dragging out the tiny canvas tool-roll, grabbing spanner and screwdriver, fumbling with the connection-joints in the torchlight beam. He stopped, looked around, and frowned. 'I need a cloth – a shield of some kind.'

Thane pulled off his jacket. 'Here.'

MacPherson nodded, used the cloth to form a shapeless mass around the spray-swept outboard, disconnected the final few screw-threads, and took a dirty but dry handkerchief from his inside pocket. He worked on for a moment or two, then nodded. 'It's done.'

'Right.' Thane bent forward. The weight of all three men so close to the stern of the dinghy had reduced its freeboard to a matter of scant inches – but the next stage was crucial. Carefully, he poured a tiny allowance of the moonshine liquor into the waiting carburetter bowl and gave a silent prayer to whatever power had responsibility for watch over peril afloat.

'Now. . . .' MacPherson yanked the starter cord. Nothing happened. 'Maybe the spark plug –'

'We haven't time. Try again, man – keep trying.'

Pull – sigh. Pull – sigh. Pull – and a cough. Pull again – and the engine howled to life.

'Get nearer the bow, mister.' Life pulsing in his boat once more seemed to seep new energy to MacPherson. 'Balance her off a bit.'

Phil Moss lurched back, settled in a crouch in his new position, and kept his torchbeam flashing landwards.

'I'm going to gamble, Chief Inspector,' declared the boatman. He spluttered as a stray dash of seawater hit his face, and went on. 'I'll steer to port, but still with the race. If we turned, we wouldn't have enough power to fight head-on against this current – but this way, we may be able to punch out a bit towards the fringe.'

Thane nodded, still in his cramped crouch, shielding the flask and carburetter, trickling the precious liquor into the bowl a few drops at a time. 'There's maybe four minutes running time in this flask,' he warned. 'Make the most of it.'

MacPherson took the control bar, jut-jawed and earnest, fingers light on the throttle, dropping his engine revs as the dinghy entered each wave-trough, increasing power on the smoother water beyond, propeller clawing the little craft on its perilous escape bid, gaining slow, precious distance.

They were near enough to The Fangs now for the moonlight to show the jagged broken teeth which waited behind the white fury of water breaking round the base of the half-tide rocks.

Muscles straining to maintain their rigid control, Thane fed more of the triple-run liquor into the carburetter bowl, tipping the flask higher now, conscious that little of its contents remained.

'There – there's a boat!' Drenched, half-forgotten, Phil Moss shouted the words from the bow, one quivering arm pointing almost straight to their port quarter.

They saw it. The continual wave-roar, the background rumble of The Fangs, drowned all sound of its engine. But, even in the miserable light, the squat, rolling bulk of the *Rock Rose* was unmistakable, a glow of light in its wheelhouse making a beacon of fresh chance, a contact with an outside world of fresh hope. Preston's boat was steering in the same direction, on a course veering in towards their battered dinghy.

'Preston's gone mad,' groaned MacPherson despairingly. 'We've one chance in a thousand as it is – every yard he comes nearer he's cutting his own safety margin.'

A spotlight flared to life from the shark-boat's masthead, its beam wavering as the *Rock Rose* pitched, then pinning on the dinghy. Now forty yards, no more, separated the two craft . . . and for the first time Thane realized that the figure in the wheelhouse was not the bronze-bearded shark fisher. Gwen Preston was there, her back jammed against the rear of the flimsy structure, her face a white blur through the spray. The motor sailer was moving clumsily, a strange black shape lashed to the craft's side, a shape still pliant enough to seem to shudder as each sea broke upon it.

Then he saw Finn Preston. The giant Viking figure was crouched for'ard on the *Rock Rose*, beside the harpoon gun, swivelling it round on its crude mounting until it seemed to be pointing straight at them. The gun's muzzle belched red flame as its black powder charge blasted a whistling harpoon projectile through the air, a thin, snaking cable flickering behind it.

The harpoon lanced scant feet above their heads then hit the water beyond, its trailing cable smacked down across the dinghy, near the bow, and began to slide.

'Grab it – grab it, man!' MacPherson screamed the words as Phil Moss lunged towards the vital line, every ounce of energy in his small, wiry frame going into a death-like grip round the cord.

'Tie it on – tie it! Och, for pity's sake' – MacPherson abandoned the tiller, hurled himself towards the bow, and came to the aid of the gasping, spray-soaked figure who was experiencing inch-by-inch agony as the cable slipped

145

through his fingers. Gwen Preston was doing her best to hold the *Rock Rose* steady – but the rope was straining, and human flesh and skin make a poor brake on nylon cable. Grabbing the free end beyond the detective, MacPherson pulled a short length inboard and wound it swiftly and scientifically round the dinghy's bow mooring ring.

'Let go now,' he bellowed in Moss's ear. Phil Moss clung on in a daze of concentration. It took a second bellow before he released hold, to nurse his rope-burned salt-stung palms.

Captive, the dinghy bobbed crabwise to the next wave. But Preston was already busy on the next stage of his rescue operation. A mechanical clamour from the *Rock Rose*'s foredeck was followed by a tauting of the nylon cable – this was the way the bearded giant brought his five-ton sharks alongside the motor sailer, and it was equally effective now. Willie MacPherson scrambled back to the stern of the dinghy, opened the outboard engine's throttle to full power, and Thane fed the last teaspoonful of alcohol fuel into the carburetter bowl.

Between them, the winch and the outboard brought the water-logged dinghy closer to the larger craft. Preston signalled, heaved a second, thicker line by hand and stood ready. As the dinghy tossed nearer, Thane recognized the black shape tied alongside the *Rock Rose* as a dead basking shark – and then, seconds before the little craft bumped into the fish's carcase, the outboard engine spluttered to a halt, its fuel exhausted.

'Now!' Preston shouted the word, one hand out-stretched. From the bow, using the second line as support, Phil Moss scrambled over the shark carcase and half-fell on to the *Rock Rose*'s deck. Willie MacPherson shoved Thane forward, the burly detective gripped the rope, stepped on to the heaving, pliant, yet lifeless body, then had his hand seized by Finn Preston and was literally yanked on to the deck above. MacPherson came last – and Finn Preston wasted no time. As the boatman reached

146

safety, the big shark fisher slashed with a long-bladed knife. The nylon line parted and the dinghy tossed free.

'Get below' – he shoved the three soaked, exhausted figures towards the wheelhouse. Phil Moss and MacPherson tumbled in and staggered down the companionway into the cabin below. Preston squeezed in behind Thane, and nodded to his wife.

'I'll take it, Gwen.'

She obeyed instantly, and as Preston's hands closed on the steering wheel the brunette went down to the cabin without a backward glance.

Thane wiped the salt water trickles from his forehead, shivering in his spray-soaked shirt and trousers, having a last glimpse of his jacket, still wrapped round the dinghy's outboard, as the little craft wallowed away.

'We're not out of it yet.' Finn Preston braced himself, feet apart, and Thane jammed himself back in the corner. 'I can't get her completely clear of The Fangs – we're too near.'

The menace of the rocks was now a scant couple of hundred yards distant, a foaming cauldron of water. The *Rock Rose* was winning away from the centre of the danger ahead, but her angled course still led towards the fringe of the jagged, ship-tearing fury.

'What can we do?' Thane knew his sole chance of staying alive depended on the skill of the bearded giant beside him.

'Gamble.' Preston spat the words. 'There's a gap, Chief Inspector. Depends on the tide – if it's too low then the bottom rocks will bacon-slice the keel. The current's fierce, and she'll take a battering. But' – he gave a grimace – 'I've got twenty foot of dead shark lashed along each side. They'll make pretty useful fenders.'

With one hand he eased the engine throttle forward a couple of notches. Outside the thin shelter of the wheelhouse glass, the seas grew wilder and more confused in pattern with each second that passed. Preston's grip was knuckle-white on the polished wood of the steering wheel, his shoulder muscles bulged his tight-fitting blue jersey. The *Rock Rose*, engine throbbing, pitched and jerked as, her whole structure sighing and creaking, she fought to achieve her master's chosen path in defiance of the sucking urge of the tidal race.

It was the little things Thane found himself noticing – the trickle of perspiration which eased a slow path down Finn Preston's brow; the quivering constancy of the needle in the compass binnacle; the miniature eddies of water which washed across the decking at their feet.

With a jerk and a plunge, the *Rock Rose* reached the boiling line of water. On either side the granite rocks pressed close and hungry, there was a grinding, grating shudder beneath their feet, the whole craft canted and swung, and a hammer-blow seemed to strike the ship's starboard quarter. Another shuddering jerk, the motor sailer shook her length with the violence of a rain-wet dog, a lighter blow, this time on the port side but further astern, and then she flew forward curtsying, lurching, rolling, but free.

Finn Preston took one hand from the steering wheel and gave a long, lung-emptying sigh. 'I could use a cigarette – then I'm going to go into a nice quiet corner and quiver like a jelly. Any objections?'

Thane shook his head. 'I'll join you . . . quiver for quiver.'

# Chapter Seven

Her ordeal at an end, the *Rock Rose* lay at anchor a half-mile south-west of Sanctuary Isle. The sea's mood had returned to placid indifference, and the broad-beamed motor sailer rocked gently and reassuringly in the slow-moving swell.

Finn Preston clattered down the companionway into the little cabin, a dark oil-smear streaking one side of his nose, and gave a nod of pleased satisfaction. 'No real damage that I can find,' he reported. 'She's lost some paintwork, there are a few more dents than we had before, and there's just a trace of a leak sprung near the stern. But she'll do – thanks to the sharks.'

Five people in the confined, dim-lit space of the cabin constituted a crowd. The mixed odours of damp, engine-oil and cigarette smoke were fighting a hard battle against the more appetizing flavours of coffee and bacon wafting from the little galley-kitchen aft.

Colin Thane leaned back on the day-couch, his head inches away from the glow of a bulkhead-mounted light. 'A pretty useful catch,' he agreed dryly. 'And lucky for us you were around. The police pension fund owes you a vote of thanks.'

Hands on hips, Preston grinned at his trio of ship-wrecked guests. Phil Moss, his hands bandaged where the rope-burns had taken their toll, was dressed in slacks and roll-necked fishing jersey both several sizes too large for his meagre frame. Willie MacPherson had protested against all suggestion of a change of clothing, and had contented himself with hanging his faded blue overalls up to dry, leaving him in slacks and shirtsleeves. Thane, however, had willingly borrowed from Preston's wardrobe and relaxed in a garish tartan shirt and a pair of white drill trousers.

'We can hardly call you a well-dressed yachting group,' declared the shark fisher. 'Not to worry, we'll soon get your own kit dried out.'

'It won't take long,' agreed Gwen Preston, emerging from the galley-space. She had a tray loaded with coffee and a massive plate of bacon sandwiches, and placed it in the centre of the cabin table. 'Help yourselves.'

They did. Even Phil Moss, ulcer temporarily forgotten, agreed that there was nothing quite like coming within a few yards of drowning to develop an appetite.

Preston munched a mouthful, washed it down with near-scalding coffee, then frowned. 'What happened out there, Thane? And don't try to tell me it was an accident. Your dinghy wasn't the only boat around the Isle tonight – I know that for a start. And Willie MacPherson doesn't take chances when he's sailing around The Fangs. Nobody who knows these waters ever would.'

'It was no accident,' agreed Thane. 'Somebody poured salt water in the dinghy's fuel tank while we were ashore.'

'Somebody!' MacPherson gave an outraged snort. 'It was that fancy-smiling devil Sonders – and I'm going to take it out of his hide soon as I get near him, bodyguard or no bodyguard.'

'Sonders' – Gwen Preston repeated the name, and glanced apprehensively across the cabin towards her husband. Preston's eyes narrowed, but the bearded giant made no comment.

'It was Sonders and his men, we can be sure of that,' said the detective. 'But the interesting thing, Mrs Preston, is that they didn't realize they were doing it to us. They thought that the dinghy was from the *Rock Rose*. They thought it was your husband who was going to end up on

150

The Fangs. And you know' – his attention flicked across to the shark fisher – 'I've a pretty good idea why. Sonders believed that Phil Moss and I were miles away, and I hope you're not going to try to tell me that it was shark-fishing that brought you to this part of the Firth in the middle of the night.'

'What else, Chief Inspector?' Finn Preston was cautious. 'You've seen the brutes for yourself – battered a bit more than they were, but still there.'

'All right, you were fishing. But that was earlier, much earlier.' Thane helped himself to another sandwich. 'You were out here for a reason which goes right back to even before Captain Tinemann's death. A reason which meant, eventually, that Edgar Hollis had to die – a reason which almost cost more lives tonight.' He paused, and signalled to his second-in-command. 'Phil, I don't like the idea of the boat being without some kind of a watch on deck. Maybe you and MacPherson could go up and keep an eye open.'

The boatman scratched his head. 'If that's a hint, Chief Inspector, I can take it on my own. No need for an escort – you'll have your privacy. Anyway, you're right. Sonders might still be prowling around in that launch of his.' With an encouraging wink to the shark-fisher, he got to his feet, went up the companionway, and closed the hatch doorway behind him.

'Willie knows part of what's going on,' said Thane. 'He guesses more. But it's better we have this talk alone, just the four of us.'

'A friendly talk – or an official questioning?' demanded Preston.

'Midway between the two,' compromised Thane. He turned to the girl standing beside him and smiled encouragingly. 'Sit down, lass. I'm not planning to throw either of you into a police cell, but the time has come for truth. You want to see Captain Tinemann's killer brought to a reckoning?'

She nodded, and settled slowly on the day couch at his

side. Finn Preston, moving with equal reluctance, squeezed on to the opposite seat beside Phil Moss.

'Let's see now. . . .' Thane rubbed his chin. 'Supposing I begin with a few facts. We know about the Armada treasure. We know that Captain Tinemann had come across some clue to its location. And, just as important, we know that the only reason Sonders brought the *Gabrielle* to these waters was that same treasure. We're also sure that Sonders or one of his yacht hands poisoned Captain Tinemann. Well, will that do for a start?'

Preston frowned down at the table-top, then looked across at his wife. They said nothing, but a silent message of understanding and agreement seemed to pass between them. The shark fisher rose, crossed the cabin, and pressed a portion of seemingly solid panelling. It moved, swung back, and he reached into the dark space beyond.

'Nearest thing to a safe we have,' he said ruefully, taking out a small oilskin-wrapped package. He tossed the package across the cabin, and Thane caught it one-handed. 'Open it,' invited the shark fisher.

Thane undid the oilskin and held the small dull-metal disc it contained nearer to the light.

'Captain Tinemann found that on the Isle, when he began to clear the blocked-up well,' said Preston, his last hint of reserve vanishing. 'Not in the well itself, but among the shingle beside it. Take a close look, Chief Inspector. That's a gold coin – a Spanish ducat, time-worn, but you can still make out the date. It was minted in the reign of Philip the Second of Spain, in 1586 – two years before the Armada sailed. There was something else, a piece of wood he found in among the well debris. Tinemann reckoned that they amounted to proof that Spaniards had landed on the Isle, and that there might be a fortune lying buried among the rocks.'

'And you were helping him try to find it?'

Finn Preston gave a nod. 'He told me almost as soon as he found the coin, and I located some dates for him, to make sure that it could have been from the Armada

152

period. But – how did Sonders find out about it? He was here with the *Gabrielle* even before the Bird Society put the captain on to the Isle as warden!'

'Blame a Swiss professor of history.' Thane sketched the strange fashion in which Professor Hundell's political research project had developed into a treasure hunt.

'So old Tinemann was right.' Preston gave a long, low whistle of surprise. 'A fortune, a genuine certain fortune – and it's over there, under some ruddy gull's nest!'

'Chief Inspector' – Gwen Preston was puzzled. Her cheeks flushed, her voice strained, she demanded, 'If you know so much, why don't you arrest Sonders and his men? Surely after what happened tonight it's the obvious thing to do?'

Thane shook his head, but it was Phil Moss who answered, making no attempt to hide his bitter annoyance. 'I'll tell you why, Mrs Preston. Because, in part, you and your husband have been darting in and out of this investigation from the word go, acting like a well-fanned smoke-screen. And the rest of it is that we've built up a case which is strong in circumstance but flimsy in fact. We need a peg to pin the whole thing together, the kind of peg that even a fast-talking defence counsel can't dislodge.' He stopped and blinked apologetically in his chief's direction.

'Go on, Phil,' agreed Thane.

'Thanks.' Detective Inspector Moss was angry, an anger which needed some safety-valve relief. 'You kept quiet about the treasure. Why? Greed, wasn't it? You knew that Royan Sonders was on the same ploy – if we'd been told about that, then Hollis's death might have been prevented. And' – he glared at Finn Preston, a terrier growling at a reluctant bear – 'why didn't you admit that Hollis came back to see you a second time the night he was killed?'

'Hey, wait a minute!' Preston was aroused now. 'We told you Hollis was here once, and went away. That's all we know.'

'Finn's telling the truth,' declared his wife. 'Say what

153

you like about us for keeping silent about the Armada gold – though I wonder how even two high-principled policemen would behave if someone waved the chance of a fortune under their noses. But we don't know if Hollis came back or not. We weren't on the *Rock Rose* for more than ten minutes after he left.'

'Eh?' Thane paused, a cigarette midway to his lips.

The young brunette nodded. 'We weren't aboard. Finn and I took the dinghy, and sneaked out to the *Gabrielle*. We had to – we were afraid Mr Hollis was beginning to realize what Captain Tinemann had discovered.' She pursed her lips, then dropped a minor bombshell in Thane's lap. 'Sonders didn't have a lookout on deck. We used oars instead of the engine, and got alongside without being seen. Then we heard them talking.'

'Who – Sonders and Hollis?' Thane barked the question.

'Sonders and Hollis,' agreed Finn Preston. 'It was a warm night, Thane. Most of the portholes on the *Gabrielle* were at least part-open, and us alongside in the dinghy, scared of every wave-splash in case it brought that whole mob of French muscle-men on deck.'

'Wait a minute.' Thane held up his hand in protest. 'You thought Hollis might have twigged the fact that you and Tinemann were looking for treasure. Was that because of the book parcel he left behind, the one you denied ever having seen?'

'It's in the bulkhead compartment,' admitted the shark fisher. 'Oh, he ranted on for a bit when he was here – keep off Sanctuary Isle, or else; that the next warden would be hand-picked and we'd be prosecuted if we even stepped ashore – that sort of thing. But it was only when we saw the parcel that we really became worried.'

'Two volumes on the Spanish Armada.' Thane sighed and shook his head. 'Let's have 'em.'

Preston once again went over to the bulkhead hiding place, and laid the brown paper parcel on the table. 'After he disappeared, well, the safest thing to do seemed to keep quiet about these books.'

'I'm more interested in what you heard when you were doing your eavesdropping act at the *Gabrielle*,' growled Thane.

'I'll tell him, Finn.' Gwen Preston moistened her lips with her tongue. 'They'd obviously been talking for some time when we reached the yacht. Sonders was being – just Sonders, full of smooth charm. We heard him say something about a cheque, but we couldn't understand that part –'

Phil Moss, a cigarette smouldering between his bandaged fingers, gave a grunt. 'Sonders sent a cheque for a thousand pounds to the Scottish Sea Bird Society. Posted it the morning after Hollis disappeared.'

'Blood money,' spat Finn Preston. 'Tell them the rest, Gwen.'

She smiled wanly. 'If I'm given the chance.' The three men sat silent as she continued, 'What we heard was enough, Chief Inspector – enough to let us know that Mr Hollis hadn't had any idea what was going on, but that Captain Tinemann had been right when he'd told us he was sure Sonders was on the same quest as ourselves. Sonders said he'd send this cheque – but that it would be worth a lot more money, both to Mr Hollis and, if he wanted it that way, to the Bird Society, if he'd make sure the right man was appointed as bird warden on the Isle. Mr Thane, he told Hollis that he wanted the run of the Isle for a week, no more. That he wouldn't disturb the sea birds, and that at the end of it he'd pay Hollis five thousand pounds for the privilege.'

It all fitted. A week would be long enough for an intensive detector-equipped search of the Isle, and Sonders, his original plan misfired, would see the proposition as a simple business investment.

Edgar Hollis, unfortunately, had seen it differently. 'He became angry,' declared Gwen Preston. 'At first he said the only thing he could do would be to put a suggestion before his committee – and Sonders just laughed and told him

155

this was a private deal or not at all. Then . . . well, Mr Hollis said he'd have to tell the police about the offer.'

'And Sonders?' Chief Inspector Thane could already guess the sequel.

The girl frowned. 'I'm not sure. We heard him say that he didn't care – that he'd go and tell one of the crew to get the speedboat ready, and he'd take Mr Hollis back to the shore.'

'And that,' growled Finn Preston, 'was our signal to get out of the way. We eased the dinghy away from the *Gabrielle*, into the Firth a bit, and stayed there until we saw the speedboat leave the yacht and then come back out from the harbour again. After that, we circled round and got back into the harbour without being seen. When you descended on us the following night, our first worry was that Hollis had told you the lot and dragged us into it. All right, it sounds cold-blooded – but I felt a lot happier when you said he'd disappeared.'

Their attitude that of being freed from a long, over-shadowing strain, there was no doubt that the Prestons' story was simple, unvarnished truth. But there might be more – more than they realized.

'After you moved the dinghy away from the *Gabrielle*, how long was it until the speedboat took Hollis ashore?' asked Thane.

Preston's bearded face twisted in concentration. 'Don't know exactly. Longer than we'd expected – perhaps fifteen minutes. We thought Sonders was maybe trying a different approach to Hollis.'

'Maybe he was,' said Thane, thinking of the harmless little ornithologist, so fiercely protective of his feathered charges. Hollis, he reckoned, would rather die than bargain over their suddenly troubled haven.

And he had died – swiftly, brutally.

'While you were in the dinghy, did you hear or see anything unusual – anyone else going ashore by boat, for instance?'

The shark fisher pondered, then shook his head. 'Nothing that I can remember. How about you, Gwen?'

'No . . .' she puzzled over the question. 'Finn said there was a seal around somewhere, but we couldn't see it.'

'What about this seal?' probed Thane. Phil Moss caught the significant tension in his companion's voice, realized the reason, and perched forward on the edge of the day-couch.

Finn Preston rough-combed his beard with the fingers of one hand. 'It was just a seal as far as I know. I heard a splash near the *Gabrielle* and thought I saw its head in the water for a moment. They sometimes come close into the harbour at this time of year.'

'This seal –' Moss took over the questioning '– it was somewhere near the *Gabrielle*, and then it headed in towards the harbour?'

'Uh-huh. Why?'

'At that distance, at night, could you tell the difference between a seal and a man in frogman's kit? Could it have been someone leaving the *Gabrielle*, coming up for a moment to get his bearings and then swimming underwater to the shore?'

Preston's eyes widened perceptibly. 'If he was wearing a black rubber cold-weather suit, yes. Is that –'

'How Hollis was killed?' Colin Thane nodded. 'It looks very much like it, Preston. Sonders stalls for time, then takes Hollis ashore and lands him where there are witnesses. Hollis walks into the darkness, heading towards your boat – Sonders told us that he was going back for his parcel. The frogman was already ashore and waiting, and you were a nice, handy suspect. They worked the frogman trick on us tonight. As for Captain Tinemann, my bet is that while the *Gabrielle* didn't go near Sanctuary Isle, Sonders used the mist that evening to cover his making a speedboat trip to the Isle. Probably his frogman pal was with him, to swim round and dampen the wood on the signal beacon while Sonders gave the captain a dose of aconite mixed in a swig of whisky.'

157

'If the captain was short of booze he'd accept a throat-wetting from the devil himself,' muttered Finn Preston. Savagely, he struck one clenched fist on the table. 'But, hell man – what do we do about it? Because I'm in this too, anyway you'll have me.'

'I was hoping you'd say that.' Thane smiled across at the angry, bearded Viking. 'Because I'll need you and your wife backing me to the limit if I'm going to get Sonders where I want him – back out on the Isle again.'

'We'll shake on that,' vowed Preston. His huge grip pumped Thane's hand, then, in gentler style, Phil Moss's bandaged fingers. 'Woman, get out the glasses – we'll drink to it!'


Two hours later, as dawn light roused the sleeping Firth of Lorne to another day, the dinghy from the *Rock Rose* grounded to rest on a sandy beach four miles south of Inverlay harbour.

'Stage one,' said Colin Thane as he stepped ashore. 'Right, let's get this under cover.' Phil Moss and Mac-Pherson joined him in heaving the open boat up the beach until it was hidden under the thick, low-lying bushes which rimmed the edge of the sand. When they were finished, the three men stood back to admire their handi-work, then set off on a trudge to the nearest telephone. It was going to be up to Argyll county police to ensure that stage two went off with equal ease.


Half an hour on from the time Colin Thane reached shore, the *Rock Rose* made her approach to Inverlay harbour. On the quayside, sleepy-eyed fishermen were already prepar-ing to sail with the incoming tide, their boats were alive with the characteristic putter of paraffin-powered engines, the first squadrons of hungry seagulls were already cir-cling a cawing pattern above.

The spluttering fizz of a red signal flare, its burst, and

the slowly descending plume of colour brought a sudden halt to the everyday preparations. First one man then another saw the ominous signal flag flying at the motor sailer's masthead – white, with a blue outer frame and a square red centre . . . letter W, in sea code a flag with only one meaning: 'I require medical assistance.'

One fleet-footed youngster went sprinting towards the harbour office telephone. A slow-gathering crowd watched as the shark boat came slowly past the trim blue and white motor yacht lying outside the harbour mouth. At the *Gabrielle's* deck-rail, Royan Sonders and one of his crew watched with apparently detached curiosity.

Ashore, the watchers were already speculating. The *Rock Rose's* deck boat had vanished, one noted. Another, sharper-eyed, gave a whistle of surprise. 'Hey, that's Preston's wife at the wheel – something must have happened to the big fellow!'

Their attention was glued to the battered, work-stained boat as it began to manoeuvre into the quayside. Nobody paid attention to the speedboat heading shorewards from the *Gabrielle*. As Preston's wife completed the difficult task of berthing the *Rock Rose* single-handed, the burly form of Sergeant Stewart pushed forward through the crowd. The Argyll County officer jumped down on to the deck of the motor sailer, threw bow and stern ropes up to the quayside where there was no lack of hands to complete the mooring, and then went into the wheelhouse. Two other uniformed police stood by above, holding back the crowd.

After a couple of minutes, Sergeant Stewart clambered up on to the quay again. He glanced around and frowned. 'No sign of that ambulance yet? Finn Preston's in a bad way – unconscious.'

'What happened, sergeant?' asked the nearest of the fishermen.

Sergeant Stewart gave a shrug. 'His wife doesn't know for sure. Seems Preston took their dinghy and went ashore on Sanctuary Isle – after seals, according to her.'

'He's shot himself then!' exclaimed his questioner.

'Mind your own dam' business, Donny MacLeod,' said the sergeant majestically. 'This iss an official matter.'

There was an instant grumble from his audience.

'All right, all right,' he gave in. 'Mrs Preston says he stayed away longer than she'd expected. She was just going to bring the *Rock Rose* in nearer the shore, when she heard him starting out from the Isle again. Then he disappeared, and she couldn't find him . . . it looked as though the dinghy's engine had failed, and the tide race starting.' He shrugged his broad, uniformed shoulders. 'The poor lass was sailing out there all night, trying to find him, almost getting pulled into the race herself. She found him on The Fangs this morning, and the boat in matchwood.'

The news brought a fresh rumble of discussion. The Fangs – any man who was dragged on to that maelstrom of water and lived was blessed with a particularly diligent guardian angel.

The fishermen gave way as the village undertaker, his black mourning rigout hastily exchanged for uniform cap and tunic, drove Inverlay's ambulance at a slow crawl along the quayside and halted beside the little vessel. He got out, opened the rear doors, and lifted the rolled-up stretcher. Being part-time ambulance driver had its advantages when you were the local undertaker. Not that he'd dream of soliciting business, of course – but it meant that when the time came you were a known face to the surviving relatives. Preston would be a heavy one – aye, it would do no harm to measure him against the notches cut most unofficially into the stretcher poles.

Then minutes later, a reinforced party of police eased the stretcher ashore from the *Rock Rose*. Finn Preston lay still and white, a bandage wrapped round his head, his eyes closed.

Weary, stumbling, his wife followed the stretcher and waited until it was placed in the back of the ambulance. She stepped in beside it and was joined by Sergeant Stewart and a constable. The doors closed, and the ambu-

160

lance driver started up his engine. Inverlay's police, he grumbled, were getting more than a little high-handed. Taking the stretcher from him, carrying out the moving themselves . . . he sighed, and jammed the gear-lever into reverse.

As the ambulance backed its way along the quayside, heading towards the road, a stocky, dark-complexioned seaman strolled away from the thinning crowd.

No one stopped him. Thane had been most specific in his orders.


The ambulance journey ended at Oban Cottage Hospital, and once again the vehicle's part-time driver fumed as his stretcher-borne patient was lifted from the ambulance and carried in to the building without his assistance being either required or requested. He swallowed his indignation and gave his standard smile of sympathy as Preston's wife hurried to follow the procession. After all, public relations was important in the funeral trade, just as much as having a clean white collar and not too limp a handshake.

Inside the hospital, the two police constables carried their stretcher down the corridor, escorted by a twinkling-eyed nurse. She knocked on a glass-panelled door, turned the handle, and waved them in, Gwen Preston following at their heels.

As the door closed again, the two policemen lowered their burden with a sigh.

'Up you get, Preston,' groaned Sergeant Stewart. 'Man, my arms are just about out of their sockets carrying you about.'

Finn Preston tossed his blanket covers aside and rose to his feet, a wide grin on his face as he greeted the four men already in the room. 'Everything okay so far?' he queried, unwinding the bandage from his head.

'Everything fine,' agreed Chief Inspector Thane. With him was Phil Moss, Inspector Davidson from the County force and, inevitably by now, Willie the boatman. 'We've had word from Inverlay – Sonders was very interested in all that happened.'

'Well, I'm glad to hear it,' growled the shark fisher. 'Now then, Chief Inspector, how about some breakfast? I'm a sick man, remember – I need regular feeding!'

'That's been organized,' grinned Thane. 'It's waiting at Inspector Davidson's place – and his wife won't thank us if we leave it to over-cook. We'll go out the back way – there are cars waiting.'

Breakfast was a leisurely affair in the police inspector's home, a bungalow set high on the hill overlooking the wooded sweep of Oban Bay.

When they'd finished, Davidson's wife, a sturdily built woman with corn-fair hair, refused all offers of help to wash up.

'From what Hugh's told me, though that's never much, you've got more important things than dishes to attend to,' she declared. 'Now, just let me get on with it.'

As the policeman's wife left the room, Willie MacPherson sighed appreciatively. 'Och, I never thought I'd be having a meal at your table, Inspector . . . but grand it was, and I'll be remembering it next time you've got me in a cell.'

'If it wasn't for a certain illicit still . . .' Davidson let the reminder settle unfinished, and turned to Thane. 'Well, sir, what's next on your programme?'

'A problem, I'm afraid.' Thane swirled the last dregs of coffee in his cup, troubled by the one apparent gap remaining in his plan. 'How can we put the *Gabrielle's* radar out of operation, and make it appear to be due to some hard-to-trace fault?'

Davidson blinked. 'That's a pretty tall order.'

'But a necessary one.' Thane finished the coffee and set down his cup. 'As I see it, Sonders had a radar watch on duty aboard the *Gabrielle* last night while he and the rest of his crew went treasure-hunting on the Isle. Now it's pretty certain that the radar didn't pick up any trace of our dinghy – but it did locate the *Rock Rose* as she cruised into the neighbourhood.'

Finn Preston nodded agreement. 'That's likely. We were steering a course to the Isle when we heard some other craft in the neighbourhood, and decided to keep our distance for a spell.'

'Then, with a radio link from the *Gabrielle* to Sonders' launch, he'd be told that another boat was nearby,' expounded Thane. 'He'd send his frogman on a scout around the shore, in case any other landing had been made, and, well, we know what happened after that. Now I want to coax Sonders back out to the Isle tonight – and he shouldn't need much encouragement if his detector gear did discover the treasure-site last night. All he has to do now is go back, do some digging, and then get every knot of speed he can out of the *Gabrielle* in quitting the area altogether.'

'Supposing he tries to check up on me with the hospital?' demanded the shark fisher.

'That's been taken care of, in detail.' Inspector Davidson permitted himself a dry chuckle of satisfaction. 'All inquirers will be told that you're still unconscious and have been transferred as an emergency case to Killearn Hospital, not far from Glasgow. There's a specialist neuro-surgical unit there, and anyone anxious enough to find out will hear you're on the danger list, that you've to undergo an operation for a fractured skull, and that it's likely to be at least a couple of days before you're well enough to talk.'

'Sonders has no real proof you know about the treasure – or that anyone else does, for that matter,' explained Thane. 'As far as he's concerned, you probably did go ashore on a seal-hunting foray. He'd get a nasty shock finding that you were still alive – but as long as he believes this story, thinks you're unconscious, and that your wife doesn't know what happened –'

'Then he still has a clear field as far as getting the treasure is concerned!' Preston had sudden full appreciation of the vice-like situation closing on their quarry.

'While I'm unconscious, he's safe. But he has to be finished and well away before I "come round" in hospital and start talking about what happened.'

'Which means he'll probably move tonight. And this time I'm going to nail him red-handed – if I can find a way of putting the *Gabrielle's* radar set out of action before he leaves.' Thane rose from the table, the puzzle a worrying problem clouding his mind. 'If you've any bright ideas, let me know.'

For Chief Detective Inspector Colin Thane it was once again the time he found the hardest of all in every case. The time for waiting, the time when he had to stop making the running and leave it to the other man to act, hoping that, faced with a carefully planned set of circumstances created for his benefit, Royan Sonders would in fact decide there was only one course of action he could take.

In the side-room placed at their disposal in Oban police station he tried hard to appear relaxed and cheerful, made an effort to concentrate on drafting the written report which should have already been on its way to Buddha Ilford at Headquarters, and found that in half an hour he'd written exactly forty-three words.

'Ach!' He scowled as the pencil point snapped short. 'Reports and more reports. Find me the man who first thought of them and –'

'And you'll tell him a thing or two, I know.' Phil Moss was suitably sympathetic. Somehow, the paper-work side of a job didn't particularly trouble Detective Inspector Moss. Colin Thane preferred the slash and parry of action, and Moss made no complaint on that score. But Thane's second-in-command could find an oddly soothing quality in the assembling of fact, the choosing of an amalgam of words which could present the bald, undramatic prose necessary for official report-sheets.

The reluctant report-writer sighed and searched the pockets of his suit for his cigarettes. Both he and Moss had

164

been glad to get back to their hotel room and change into the spare clothing brought north from the city by special car – something else for Buddha Ilford to growl about, no doubt.

'Phil' – he held out the packet, then lowered it as the telephone by his side gave a long peal. He picked up the receiver, and gave a grunt. 'Thane here.'

'Davidson, at the hospital.' The prim tone of the Argyll inspector's voice was magnified by the metallic echo of the line. 'Well, it's started. Sonders phoned from Inverlay a few moments ago – the casualty sister took the call. After she told him the tale about Finn Preston being moved, he wanted to know if he could contact Gwen Preston – said he wanted to find out any way in which he could help.'

'He's wasting no time,' said Thane softly. 'Anything else?'

'Perhaps' – Davidson hesitated. 'About your radar problem, Chief Inspector. I've just remembered a case we had locally. A fourteen-year-old boy, charged with malicious damage to Post Office property.'

'Eh?' Thane glanced despairingly at his companion.

'He was sabotaging telephones,' explained Davidson quickly, sensing the impatience at the other end of the wire. 'A very simple method – he stuck an ordinary pin through the lead wires. It shorted the phone, knocked it out of action though the equipment hadn't been touched. I thought you might be interested.'

'You thought?' Thane bellowed his delight. 'It's perfect. All we've got to do is work the same sort of dodge on the yacht. Davidson, some day at this rate you're going to be Chief Constable, or a bookie. It takes brains to be a bookie. Bless you, man.'

He slammed down the receiver and thumped the desk-top. 'Phil, think up a nice excuse, a nice innocent reason, why a posse of cops have to go aboard the *Gabrielle*. Nice and peaceful now, nothing that would upset our Mr Sonders.' He was heading for the doorway.

'Hey – what are you going to do?' Phil Moss was startled.

'See a pin and pick it up, all the day we'll have ruddy good luck,' rhymed Thane. 'Get thinking – and that's an order!'

The police Jaguar reached Inverlay at noon and drew up outside the police station to unload its passengers – Thane, Moss, the stolidly unshakeable figure of Sergeant Stewart and Willie MacPherson.

'Everything clear, sergeant?' asked Thane.

Stewart gave a slow nod. 'I wait fifteen minutes, sir, then come out. I know the rest.'

'Good.' Thane felt a bubbling sense of approaching triumph. 'Right, Willie, lead the way.'

'And glad I am to be getting back to my own boat,' declared the boatman as, leaving the sergeant, they crossed the street and walked over to the harbour. 'Which reminds me, Chief Inspector, there will be a wee question of compensation for my cousin's dinghy. A good dinghy it was, and hard to replace. Worth every penny of fifty pounds.'

'Especially with its gold-plated engine,' grunted Phil Moss sardonically as they reached the quayside. 'Come off it, Willie. You ruddy Highlanders are all the same. The mangiest farm animal gets hit by a car, and immediately it becomes the finest pedigree beast in the country. That boat was on its last legs – if he gets twenty quid for its loss he'll be lucky.'

'Forty –'

'Twenty,' growled Moss.

'Och well, thirty pounds is better than nothing,' said the boatman blithely. 'Watch now as you come down – the ladder rungs can be slippery.' He began climbing down from the quayside to his launch below.

'It's piracy!' Detective Inspector Moss made a last protest, then followed him down. Thane cast off the launch's mooring ropes, then clambered down to where Mac-Pherson was holding the boat in to the quayside until he was aboard.

The launch growled out of the harbour and made short work of the little distance to the *Gabrielle's* off-shore mooring. Willie MacPherson brought it smartly alongside the companionway ladder and hailed the deckhand who peered down at them from above.

'It's the police, wanting a word with your skipper.'

The two detectives waited in the launch while it bobbed, engine throbbing, close in under the yacht's hull. After a minute, Royan Sonders himself appeared above.

'Come aboard,' he invited. 'This is a surprise visit, Chief Inspector.'

'Thanks.' Thane turned to the boatman. 'All right, Willie, you can go back into harbour. No sense in you waiting out here – but come for us in about an hour.'

'An hour it is, Mr Thane,' MacPherson acknowledged. As soon as his two passengers had boarded the *Gabrielle* he started the launch buzzing on its return journey.

'Sorry about this, Mr Sonders,' apologized Thane as he reached the main deck, Moss just behind him. 'This is one of these occasions when we can't make formal appointments.'

The paunchy dark-haired South African raised an eyebrow. 'That sounds ominous for someone.'

'It is.' Thane's voice was grim. 'Maybe you saw the *Rock Rose* coming in this morning. Finn Preston was aboard, badly injured.'

A flicker of caution crossed the other man's face. 'Yes, I did,' he agreed. 'I heard he'd been almost drowned when his dinghy was swept on to The Fangs.'

'They've moved him to a brain surgery hospital further south,' said Phil Moss. 'His wife's gone with him.'

'I feel sorry for Gwen Preston,' declared Thane. 'But Mr Sonders, you may as well know that I've got a man at Preston's bedside. If he comes through the operation he's having about now, then I'm charging Preston with murder – the murder of Edgar Hollis.'

'But' – Sonders' surprise was genuine. 'Why? I mean, what motive did he have?'

'That's what we've been finding out in Oban,' said Thane sombrely. 'Preston is in debt up to his neck. Hollis warning him off the Isle meant an end to his seal-killing there, made his financial position desperate. You were right about the parcel, Mr Sonders – Hollis left it on the *Rock Rose*, and one of the local officers found it hidden aboard after Preston was taken off to hospital.'

'I . . . see.' Sonders rubbed his chin. 'And where do I fit in?'

Thane glanced around. 'Maybe we'd better talk about this in more privacy. Could we use your day-cabin?'

Sonders nodded, and they followed him to the little cabin behind the yacht's wheelhouse bridge. He closed the door once they had entered. 'Sit down, gentlemen. Well, Chief Inspector?'

'Inspector Moss and I want to take a formal statement from you – just going over what you told us about Hollis's visit.'

Phil Moss produced notebook and pencil, and for the first time Sonders noticed the bandages on his hands. 'Nothing serious, I hope?'

'Acid burns,' said Moss easily. 'I knocked over a test tube rig in the Scientific Bureau laboratory – they won't take long to heal.' He held the pencil ready over the opened notebook.

'Chief Inspector – I was wondering. If Preston killed Hollis, then what about Captain Tinemann's death?' Sonders made an apologetic gesture. 'It's probably not the best time to ask, but –'

'We're still working on that,' said Thane. 'Preston may face both charges. Now, if you'd just start by telling us of your meeting with Hollis on the quayside . . .'

Obediently, Sonders settled into his story, Thane sitting opposite him while Phil Moss wrote busily in the faraway corner. The yacht owner reached the half-way stage of his account, then broke off with a frown as there was a sharp knock on the cabin doorway. It opened, and one of the deck hands looked in.

'Boat coming 'longside, sir,' he reported laconically. 'There is a policeman aboard, signalling.'

'Chief Inspector?'

Thane shook his head. 'I wasn't expecting it. Let's go and see, Mr Sonders. Inspector Moss can probably use a break to catch up on his notes.'

'I'll wait,' nodded Moss.

'All right,' agreed Sonders. He and Thane followed the crewman out of the cabin, leaving the door ajar behind them.

Phil Moss waited until he heard the noisy roar of the launch engine as it revved almost alongside the *Gabrielle*, then the sound of shouted voices. He laid down the notebook and pencil, opened the doorway, glanced out, saw all was clear, and crossed over to the wheelhouse. Another swift glance around, he bent low beside the radar set, pulled the tiny, plain-metal pin from his lapel, felt along the complex multi-coloured harness of wiring at the rear of the set, located the exact spot he wanted, and rammed the pin home till the tiny round stub of its head was almost invisible.

He was back in the deckhouse, notebook in hand, when Thane and Sonders returned a few moments later.

'Never mind the statement,' said Thane briefly. 'We won't need it now.'

'Huh?'

'Sergeant Stewart's in the launch alongside. Finn Preston died during the operation.' As Moss put away his notebook, Thane turned to the yacht owner. 'Well, it's maybe better this way, Mr Sonders – for his wife, anyway.'

'I think you are right.' Sonders allowed relief into his voice. 'And now, I suppose, you've got other work ahead.'

Thane nodded. 'We'll need to get ashore right away.' Sonders followed them out of the cabin and along the deck to the companionway.

'Chief Inspector, I suppose I'd better mention it, in case you needed me again – I was planning to leave Inverlay fairly soon. Not for good, of course, but for an extended cruise, further north among the islands. You'd have no objections?'

'None whatever.' Thane stopped, one hand on the companionway guardrope. 'I don't think we'll need to trouble you again – pleasant sailing.'

The rest of the daylight hours passed quietly, except for one brief telephone call from Thane's post office contact. Royan Sonders had come ashore and despatched another telegram to his bunkering agent.

'GABRIELLE E.T.A. CLYDE FROM 11.00 HOURS TOMORROW. REQUEST STAND BY OIL FUEL BUNKERING AS ARRANGED.'

# Chapter Eight

The *Gabrielle* sailed at dusk. There was one long farewell blast from her klaxon horn as the motor yacht's long silhouette steered across the mouth of Inverlay harbour, lights gleaming on her bridge where Sonders was visible at the wheel. The throb of her diesels loudened and quickened, the sea churned around her stern as she gathered way, and she headed out into the Firth, steering a northerly course which would take her on a wide loop round the west coast of Mull.

In twenty minutes she had vanished from sight, swallowed up by the deepening gloom.

Colin Thane sipped a mug of near-scalding tea, checked his wristwatch, and glanced yet again at the group assembled in the room. It was 1 a.m., the *Gabrielle* had been at sea for two hours, and his members of the cast were poised for their parts in what, he hoped, would be the last act of the action around Sanctuary Isle.

Ten in all – himself and Phil Moss; Davidson with Sergeant Stewart and three hand-picked uniformed constables; and then their three civilian aides, Willie MacPherson, Preston and finally, Gwen Preston, who had refused point-blank to be left out of the reckoning.

The telephone before him was now their final control, a link through the R.A.F. Coastal Command station at distant Kinloss with a four-engined Shackleton reconnaisance aircraft beating a high-altitude patrol many miles away, its airborne radar, sensitive enough to pick up the conning tower of a surfaced submarine at extreme range, now used for a more unusual role . . . a through-the-night shadowing of the *Gabrielle* from a distance which would yield no betraying roar from the mighty pull of her Rolls Royce Griffon engines.

For the crew of Shackleton Able-Charlie it was a welcome break from the normal monotony of their maritime sentry-duty. For Thane, the plane's presence, laid on as a result of Buddha Ilford's direct approach to Coastal Command, meant a minute-by-minute check on the motor yacht's movements.

From Inverlay the *Gabrielle* had remained on her westerly course for almost an hour. But then, from a point close to the extreme west tip of Mull, she had swung first south then east, almost retracing the same course back into the Firth of Lorne.

The last message from the Shackleton had placed the yacht six miles distant from Sanctuary Isle travelling at reduced speed and keeping well to the fringe of the normal coastal channel.

The telephone pealed again, and he grabbed the receiver, conscious of the sudden hush throughout the room.

'R.A.F. control Kinloss here,' drawled the voice at the other end of the line. 'This looks like it, old boy. Able-Charlie's been on the blower again – your bandit type is now stationary off the north-west shore of Sanctuary Isle.'

The waiting was over – Thane breathed a long sigh of relief. 'Thanks, Kinloss. And thank the Shackleton crew for me, too, will you?'

'A pleasure,' acknowledged Kinloss control. 'And good luck.'

Thane replaced the receiver. 'Sonders has anchored behind the Isle,' he told his audience. 'Well, what more do you want? Let's go.'

MacPherson's open launch in tow, the *Rock Rose* stole out of harbour a few minutes later. Her navigation lights

172

blinked out once clear of the harbour mouth, and Finn Preston spun the wheel to swing her bows south.

'Weather's all right,' mused the shark fisher. 'Wind from the south-west, fair amount of moonlight but not too much, and a good couple of hours at least before the tidal race gets under way out at The Fangs.'

By his side, Thane murmured appreciation of the last point. He still had all too clear a memory of the pounding terror of the previous night.

'Funny to think of it, Sonders out on the Isle digging up a fortune.' Preston gave the detective a sidelong glance. 'Do you think it's really there, Thane?'

'Almost four hundred years is a long time.' Thane listened for a moment to the muffled rhythm of the boat's engine, the faint, restless background of the sea. 'Yes, I think it is – and intact. Probably not the sky-high amount most people dream about when they hear the word "galleon." But a fortune just the same.'

'And what happens to it now? Once you take over from Sonders, I mean?'

'Government property. Some of it may go to a museum, I suppose. The rest –' Thane shrugged. 'What does any government do with surplus cash? Spend it. There's to be no unofficial souvenir hunting, Preston, if that's what you're suggesting.'

'The thought might have crossed my mind,' admitted the bearded shark fisher, his eyes twinkling in the gloom. 'What I keep remembering are the words Diego Vega used about the wreck. "We who survived fulfilled our charge and reached the blessed isle of sanctuary –" How does it go on again?'

'They placed the six chests "In the keeping of both land and water, where grey sentinels keep watch beside a place of rest." Well, grey sentinels or not, Sonders is out there now. How much longer till we pick up your dinghy?'

'Just a little way more,' Preston assured him. 'A matter of minutes, that's all.'

The *Rock Rose* throbbed on, following a course roughly

173

parallel with the shore, only about two hundred yards out. The faint cloud screen on the moon couldn't prevent enough light filtering through to make each salient detail of the coastline clearly visible. As the motor sailer rounded yet another headland, Willie MacPherson gave a low call from the stern. Preston answered with a swift wave of his hand, throttled back, and the *Rock Rose* slowed until she barely drifted with the waves.

MacPherson pulled the towed launch alongside, two of the uniformed constables followed him aboard her, they cast off, and the launch headed shorewards. After a spell, the launch purred out to the *Rock Rose* once more, this time towing Finn Preston's dinghy, retrieved from its hiding-place.

'Want to take it aboard?' queried Thane.

Preston shook his head. 'Not worthwhile. We'll tow 'em both.'

The men from the launch once more on board, the launch and dinghy tied in line astern, Preston's motor sailer veered on a new course, steering with the shore directly astern. Below deck, in the tiny cabin where every porthole was blacked out, Phil Moss, Inspector Davidson and Gwen Preston played a game of three-handed poker for matchstick stakes. Inevitably, Moss was losing.

The approach to the Isle was to a plan Thane had worked out in careful consultation with both Finn Preston and MacPherson, a wide loop taking them well below the sleeping menace of The Fangs and ending at a point a good mile north and west of their final objective, the anchored *Gabrielle*. From there on, the last leg could spell success or failure. The yacht's radar eye might be blinded, but she could still serve as a floating warning-post.

Time would tell. Thane leaned back in the motor sailer's wheelhouse, letting his body roll with each wave that swayed the little craft.

Finn Preston swore softly, took one hand off the wheel, and pointed ahead. 'Too bad I can't put in a spot of work tonight. Look at 'em. It would be like shooting china ducks at a fun-fair.'

In the moonlit water ahead, the big black triangular fins dotted the surface like so many sailing-boats. They moved slowly, effortlessly, as the basking sharks, powered by smooth, unhurried strokes of muscular tails, cruised forward feeding as they went. Thane counted fully thirty of the huge fins, each one a full-grown basking shark, and then gave up.

Preston eased the wheel a point to port to avoid the slow-moving monsters. 'They often drift around in a herd – maybe they like the company,' he said. 'You know, some of the old- timers swear they've watched four, maybe five hundred of the brutes on the move, swimming along like a ruddy army of amphibious tanks.'

Gradually, the sharks were left astern. Preston stayed silent now, concentrating on calculating his position by a mixture of compass bearing, the distant lighthouse-flash from the Isle, and plain, old-fashioned seat-of-the-pants navigation. At last he was satisfied, spun the wheel vigorously to starboard and then, as the *Rock Rose* answered her helm, cut the boat's engine altogether.

The sudden silence was a clear signal to the others on board. Gwen Preston emerged from the cabin and took over the wheel. Sergeant Stewart and the three uniformed constables clustered for'ard, changing their regulation boots for thin, rubber-soled plimsoles. Thane ducked down into the cabin and joined Phil Moss and Davidson in a similar change of footwear, while above them they could hear the faint rumble of pulley-blocks.

By the time they came on deck again, the *Rock Rose* was once more under way, but this time she gained her power from the wind-filled expanse of her newly-hoisted mainsail, the red canvas dark against the sky, only the faint groan of the sail-boom, the creak of masthead ropes and the occasional faint crackle from her now cooling engine to compete with the soft swishing as her stubby bow pushed its way through the water.

This was Finn Preston's way to hunt a shark – and Thane could think of no better application than its present use. At a steady, silent five knots the *Rock Rose* steered her course for the north shore of Sanctuary Isle, her two-boat train bobbing behind on their tow-lines. For'ard by the unmasked harpoon gun, her tall muscular skipper stood wide-legged, a battered but powerful pair of night-glasses trained ahead.

Thane moved up beside him. 'Anything yet?'

'We're about half a mile off the Isle,' grunted Preston. 'Wait a minute' – he made a minute adjustment to the lenses' focus and tried again, whistling thinly through his teeth.

'Well?'

'Patience, man,' growled the shark fisher. 'Aye, I've got her. Almost dead ahead and about five hundred yards off shore. No lights. Distance, about that half-mile. We can sneak in a bit closer yet.' He lowered the night-glasses and glanced approvingly skywards. 'If the cloud holds as it is, we'll be all right.'

The *Rock Rose* nuzzled her way on, while Thane strained his eyes for a first glimpse of the yacht ahead and wished hopefully that Preston would pass him the night-glasses. He still hadn't seen faintest trace of a silhouette when Preston gave another grunt.

'That'll do us. Here' – the glasses were shoved into his hand, and the shark-fisher hurried aft to join Willie MacPherson in the slow, gentle lowering of the mainsail. As the canvas folded downwards, the *Rock Rose* lost way settling once again into her drifting roll. Night-glasses to his eyes, Thane now clearly picked out the darkened bulk of the yacht then swung the glasses towards the Isle's shore, on to the flash automatic beacon-light, and then back to sea. If there was movement anywhere between, he couldn't spot it.

He turned back to the wheelhouse. Their tow of small craft had been dragged alongside, and two of the uniformed constables were already aboard the dinghy. Ignoring the outboard engine, they each had an oar in position, rowlocks muffled with strips of cloth.

'Okay, Phil?'

Detective Inspector Moss popped a bismuth tablet into his mouth, tucked it into one cheek, and nodded. He lowered himself into the dinghy, the tow-line was cast off, and two oars dipped gently and smoothly into the water.

The little boat slid away, and aboard the *Rock Rose* they heard only the softest of sighs from the rowlock bindings, the faint rippling splash as oar blades slid in and out of the water. Even these sounds died after a few yards, and the dinghy made silent, ghost-like progress into the darkness.

Then minutes passed before a signal torch blinked three times in their direction from the *Gabrielle's* deck. By the third flash, Willie MacPherson had his launch engine started and running at a quiet tick-over. As soon as the last man of his section was aboard he had the boat throbbing a whispering path away from the motor sailer, across to the silent, darkened yacht.

Phil Moss was waiting at the foot of the *Gabrielle's* companionway ladder as the launch purred alongside. The two County constables were enough of a force to leave aboard Sonders' craft, and Detective Inspector Moss was determined he wasn't going to be left out of what lay ahead. Several hands reached out to help him aboard, and he was still regaining his balance in his new surroundings as MacPherson swung the boat away again.

'A nice piece of work, Phil,' congratulated Thane as his second-in-command settled down beside him 'Got what we want?'

'Uh-huh. There was just the one man aboard – Gino, the cook-steward. I managed to sneak up on him before he could even thumb the klaxon button.' Moss chuckled grimly. 'He talked, as soon as he heard we knew about the treasure – and when I suggested that Sonders wasn't going to be alone on these murder charges. The *Gabrielle's* launch is over by the landing place – Sonders isn't due back until he finds the treasure or an hour before daybreak, which ever comes first. And he'll tell us quite a lot when we've time to listen!' He glanced round their small company, picking out faces in the gloom. Thane and the boatman, Davidson, Sergeant Stewart and the third uniformed constable – 'Where's Preston?'

'On the *Rock Rose*, with his wife,' Thane told him. 'Preston's got his harpoon gun loaded, and swears he'll nail Sonders' boat if it tries to make a getaway. Willie . . .'

'Aye?' The boatman turned towards him.

'Can you land us on this side of the Isle, near to the south end? And keep it quiet?'

The boatman nodded. 'Just like a wee salmon-poaching job,' he promised, ignoring Inspector Davidson's stiffening disapproval.

True to his word, the launch crept in towards the shore, nosed its way round a jutting outcrop of rock, and touched bottom without the engine's note once rising.

'Stay with her, Willie,' murmured Thane. 'And keep your eyes open.' Then he followed the others as they splashed through the few inches of water to the start of the sloping beach. The lighthouse beacon flash made it easy to find their bearings and they moved forward, each man praying he wouldn't be the one to disturb one of the island's teeming bird population, enough on its own to set off a general chain-action of noisy alarm.

Colin Thane led his five-man team forward until he gauged they were halfway along the length of the Isle. The well and its treasure site still lay to the other side of the beacon light, but there was a nearer objective to hand. He signalled, and the others sank down on the rocky ground beside him.

'We're near the landing place,' he murmured. 'Sonders may have left a guard on his launch, but one way or another, let's take it out of the reckoning.'

Sergeant Stewart gave a quiet cough. 'My turn, sir,' he whispered firmly. 'Time the County had a chance.'

'On your way then,' agreed Thane.

The sergeant took off his uniform cap with its brightly polished badge, laid it on the ground beside them, then moved off with a stealth which few if any of Inverlay's population would have believed possible from a man of his bulk.

The others lay waiting, ears straining, shifting their positions a little to try to find some scant degree of temporary comfort among the stones and boulders. Once, they heard the startled cry of a seabird, smothered almost before it began, and froze, dreading its spread. But the silence was otherwise unbroken until there was the faintest crunch of feet on rock and Stewart crawled back out of the darkness.

'No guard on the boat, sir,' he reported. 'I cut the spark plug leads wi' my knife – they'll no get it away again without a tow.' He brushed a few feathers from his tunic, and shook his head. 'Sorry about that bird, sir – I didn't like doing it. But it was the only way; it was right under m' nose.'

They rose up again and headed forward, paying more attention to cover as they neared, then passed, the automatic light, crouching motionless each time its signal flashes flared out from the top of the white tower.

A patch of high wild grass and thistle was next. Thane winced as, crawling forward, a thistle stem raked a stinging path across his cheek. Around him, an occasional hiss of breath showed that the others were being equally unfortunate. Then, thankfully, they were through, on the bare stretch of granite rock which overlooked the site of the old well.

Gesturing the others to follow, Thane wriggled forward on his stomach, glaring angrily behind him at the luckless uniformed constable as the latter's tunic belt buckle grated against one section of the rock. Not that the noise mattered too much now. On ahead, they could hear the murmur of voices and the occasional clink of metal on stone. Torches blinked, and one steady, shielded beam focussed on a shallow hole excavated midway between the old well and the ruined fragment of long-ago building beside it.

They lay against the cold granite, waiting while a patch of dark cloud cleared its obscuring tail-plumes from the moon. As the pale white light beamed down, for the first time, they could clearly see the men below. All four were there, Sonders nearest the excavation, peering into it. One man was beside him, shovel in hand, and the other two were sitting on the edge of the well parapet, resting. Sonders' voice cracked an order and they shuffled forward, ready to restart.

'Seen enough?' Inspector Davidson muttered the words inches from Thane's ear.

'Uh-huh.' The drop ahead was an easy enough jump of only six feet or so. Thane made up his mind. 'You and Stewart get round to the right flank – if they break for it, they'll probably try that way, towards the landing place. I'll give you a couple of minutes to position, then Moss and I will go in with your other man.'

Davidson nodded, inched back, and tapped the sergeant on the shoulder. The two men crawled off to the right while Thane gestured Moss and the constable closer.

'Got your whistle handy, son?'

The man patted his tunic pocket and grinned.

'Right. We're going down there in a moment – and I want you to have your baton in one hand and that whistle in the other. Blow it until you feel your eyeballs are going to pop out – I want to give these characters the surprise of their lives, be right in among them before they know what's happening.'

Another cloud was drifting over the moon. Thane let it take its course, listening to the noise of work coming from the well-site below, hearing Sonders' voice urge his men on to some new effort. The South African wasn't locating his treasure as swiftly as he might have expected.

The cloud started to thin, and he rose to his feet, Phil Moss and the constable following his example. The moon slid back into view. . . .

'Sonders, we've come for you!' Thane bellowed the words, jumped from the granite ledge, landed clumsily below, but kept going. Two thuds behind him showed the others were at his back, and the shrill wheep of the police whistle tore the air. Its effect was even more startling – a screaming, terrified mass of birds rose in a thunder storm of wing-beats, a thousand and then thousands more joining them in a shrilling, bewildered mass which visibly blackened the night.

The *Gabrielle's* crew stood deafened and bewildered for a few precious seconds, then, as the three policemen burst upon them, reacted in their different ways. One, squat and swarthy, whirled his shovel above his head and sliced it sword-fashion.

Thane threw himself to one side to dodge the blurring metal shovel-edge – and a moment later a flying figure in police blue hurtled forward to take the crewman in a knee-level tackle which sent him crashing.

Another of Sonders' men was made of weaker clay. He dropped his shovel with a clatter on the rocks, made a dive in the direction of the landing place, and then skidded to a sudden standstill as Inspector Davidson materialized in front of him. The Argyll inspector snapped a judo lock on the man, twirled him round, and dragged handcuffs from his pocket. Sergeant Stewart came charging forward to the main mêlée, where Phil Moss was struggling with the last of the yacht hands, whose one ambition seemed to smash an iron bar over his head, while beside him the Argyll constable was still engaged in a rolling, punching brawl with the former shovel-wielder.

Thane passed them by, intent on only one target – Sonders. The South African was running, but in the opposite direction to the landing place, heading for the bleak seal rocks of the north shore, scrambling with wild determination over boulders and shingle.

He reached one giant granite block, turned, raised one arm, and Thane dropped for cover as flame lanced from a gun muzzle. The bullet tore jagged splinters from a rock scant inches above his head, and whined off into the night. Sonders fired two more shots from the automatic then turned and ran again, sprinting over the shingle, weaving between the larger rocks.

Once again Thane began to close the gap. Gasping for breath, Sonders stopped, blasted another bullet as his pursuer dived for shelter, then bolted again.

Behind him, Thane heard the sound of hurrying reinforcements. But there was no time – Sonders knew where he was heading, and there could be only one answer, the little speedboat, the one factor they'd forgotten. The burly, city-suited detective forced himself on in a new, frantic pace, then skidded, throwing himself sideways as Sonders turned, fired a shot which clipped a grazing path through the flapping cloth of Thane's jacket, and then dashed the last few feet to the water's edge.

The speedboat was there, and Sonders hurled himself aboard, the gun muzzle pointing unwaveringly in Thane's direction while with his free hand he fumbled to loosen the mooring rope.

Colin Thane mustered his strength for that final rush forward, a primitive red-haze fury blinding him to the certainty that Sonders' next shot would be at a range which couldn't miss. He lunged, and at the same instant a small, wiry figure crashed into him from behind, knocking him off balance, throwing him hard on to the shingle.

Sonders' last shot whined over their heads, the gun clicked uselessly, and he hurled it away as the speedboat's twin outboards fired to life. The boat churned stern first from the shore, then swung round, the outboards reaching a new, bellowing peak, a foaming bow-wave starting to rise as it carved its path out to sea.

'Sorry, Colin – but I never did believe in people doing things the hard way.' Phil Moss rose to his feet, an apologetic, almost sheepish expression on his face.

Thane winced as he got up from the shingle. 'What the hell' – he began, uncontrolled anger in his voice. He stopped short, gave a sigh, and nodded. 'Thanks, Phil.'

They stared out to sea, straining their eyes to follow the white phosphorescent wake of the speedboat's path as it spread its widening trail in the moonlight. Phil Moss frowned as his ears picked up the sound of another engine growling a new, heavier note somewhere out beyond the rasping buzz of the speedboat.

Out on the Firth a narrow, brilliant beam of light suddenly flamed to life, swung a raking path over the wavetops, retraced its path, and pinned its glare on Sonders' fast-moving craft. Finn Preston's *Rock Rose* had entered the scene, the broadbeamed motor sailer moving in at an angle in an attempt to cut off the speedboat's escape path.

'He hasn't a hope,' declared Phil Moss gloomily. 'That thing Sonders is in could run rings round him from now till next spring.'

Already the *Rock Rose's* chances were lessening as the speedboat streaked for the open firth beyond. Finn Preston played his last card in a final attempt to stop the runaway. The shark-hunter's harpoon gun bellowed its dull menace, its razor-tipped projectile screamed across the water – and for once, Preston missed. The *Rock Rose's* searchlight still held the speedboat, but it was now plainly only a gesture. Sonders half-turned to jeer, and then, from the shore and on the motor sailer alike, they saw the full horror of what followed.

The light beam showed a tall black sail-like triangle in the water ahead – and beyond it, another and another. The slow-moving armada of basking sharks were at last passing the Isle.

Sonders looked ahead, saw the first huge fin looming almost under his bow, practically turned the speedboat over in a frantic water-skid to avoid the great grey-black hulk lying inches below the surface, missed it, used every ounce of energy he had to haul the boat round again to avoid the threat of a second fin almost dead ahead, and left the speedboat bow pointing dead centre at another of the tall sail-like triangles.

Thirty feet of basking shark exploded out of the sea as

the boat rammed it at a minimum of twenty knots. The searchlight from the *Rock Rose* glinted on the underside of the lightweight hull as it was tossed into the air like a matchbox, a rag-doll figure catapulting from it as it fell back into the water. All around, the sea boiled with the frantic motion of the herd of giant fish as their great tails, tails which could smash in the side of a fair-sized boat, sent them diving and turning in panicking flight.

Somewhere in the midst of that herd of giants, giants with great tea-strainer mouths which could only feed on tiny specks of plankton, Royan Sonders died. By fear and by drowning.

On shore, Thane and Moss watched the last of the triangle fins disappear and saw the *Rock Rose's* light remain stationary as Finn Preston recovered the man's body. As the light flicked out, they turned back to the well and the excavation site.

It was there that they realized the full irony of Sonders' death. The three captured crewmen, handcuffed together, stood sullen and silent to one side of the deep hole they had cleared.

'Take a look,' invited Inspector Davidson, training his torch into its depth.

The light shone on the white bones of a skeleton, a skeleton wearing the rusted, but still recognizable remains of a Spanish breast-plate, only the hilt remaining of the sword by his side, the metal helmet by his feet in a slightly better state of preservation.

'That's all?' queried Thane in startled disbelief.

'Nothing underneath it, if that's what you mean,' said Davidson. 'A couple of layers of stone, and then bedrock. I tried Sonders' mine detector round about – there's not another metal reaction in the area.'

'But the Armada treasure' – Phil Moss was bewildered.

Thane shrugged. 'There are people who get paid for worrying about that sort of thing. We've got enough on our plate, Phil. Once Preston brings the *Rock Rose* in, we'll take this bunch and their gear back to the mainland. Sonders' yacht can stay where it is till daylight.'

For Colin Thane, the next few days were satisfactory in all but one respect.

He tidied up both murders. A few last crumbs of the aconite root were found aboard the *Gabrielle* when she was brought into harbour. Of her crew of four, three soon talked to escape from the shadow of a possible murder charge. Sonders and their fourth companion, Peroz, the stocky, swarthy character who had tried to split Thane's skull with the shovel, had been responsible for both killings. It was Peroz, the frogman, who had gone to Sanctuary Isle with the South African. While Sonders had given Captain Tinemann a drink of aconite-loaded whisky from his flask, Peroz had been at the south end of the island, damping the driftwood beacon. It was Peroz, too, they declared, who had swam ashore and had killed Edgar Hollis as he walked along the darkened quayside towards Finn Preston's boat.

The frogman maintained a bitter silence while the trio piled accusations against him.

'Well, it's your turn now,' Thane told him. 'You've been cautioned and charged – any statement?'

The man shrugged. 'It is jus' such a pity The Fangs did not have you the night I damage your dinghy.'

'And the rest?'

'Is true.'

But the mystery of the treasure remained long after the Spanish seaman's remains had been brought ashore to a new resting place in Inverlay's tiny cemetery. While the Scottish Sea Bird Society fought a constant battle to regain its rights and eject all strangers, team after team of experts and archaeologists roamed the rocks of Sanctuary Isle – all without success.

Two months later Finn Preston told his friends in Inverlay he'd decided to move on to new sea-pastures. He and

185

his wife sailed the *Rock Rose* out of harbour one morning and didn't return.

Another four months passed, and three days before Christmas a small, heavily-wrapped airmail package post-marked Miami, Florida arrived on Chief Inspector Thane's desk at Millside Division in Glasgow. The writing on the outside was unfamiliar, and he ripped it open with mounting curiosity.

Inside was a smaller, tissue-wrapped packet, a news-paper cutting and a brief, handwritten note. Curiosity mounting, he unfolded the cutting, glanced at the heading, then sat back and swore non-stop for the next fifteen seconds.

'UNDERWATER EXPLORER LOCATES GALLEON TREASURE IN SUNKEN WRECK – SCOT AND WIFE HIT SUBMARINE JACKPOT.

'Mr Finn Preston, who three months ago began a series of underwater surveys in the Gulf of Mexico after sailing his ex-shark boat the *Rock Rose* across the Atlantic with his attractive wife Gwen as his sole companion, agreed today that he has salvaged what he describes as "a small for-tune" in gold from a wrecked galleon lying in shallow water several miles off the southern edge of the Florida coast . . .'

Thane groaned and lit a cigarette before he could find the courage to read on.

'He found the gold hoard while on a skin-diving exploration of a previously known and charted wreck earlier declared worthless by other divers.

'In an exclusive interview, Mr Preston said, "I was pok-ing around in the hold when I dislodged a section of rotted bulk-head – the gold was hidden behind it. I estimate the total value of the hoard, mainly in old Spanish ducats from the mid-sixteenth century, at a minimum of one million dollars."'

Thane put down the cutting, refusing to read more. He picked up the note next. It was short, friendly, and cheer-fully sardonic.

'Dear Chief Inspector,

'I thought you might like to know of our stroke of luck, which might be called twisting the long arm of coincidence.

'At the same time, I thought I'd pass on a theory of mine. The night we brought Sonders' body back from Sanctuary Isle I forgot to bring that mine-detector ashore. Gwen and I weren't particularly sleepy, so we took a quiet trip out to The Fangs (you'll remember how easy it is to land there at low tide). I tried the mine detector on one or two spots, out of curiosity, and got what seemed to be a metallic action in one particular cleft.

'I wonder . . . maybe that's what the Spaniard meant when he wrote "we fulfilled our charge and reached the blessed isle . . ." Perhaps they buried the stuff there and then on The Fangs at low tide, before they crossed to the Isle.

'Maybe the Armada chests are still there. If there are a few items short, well, maybe it's just as well I've got my own galleon out here! Enclosed is a genuine Gulf of Mexico type souvenir.'

Finn Preston's signature scrawled across the foot of the note. Thane opened the tissue-wrapped package and looked long and hard at the gleaming gold coin dated 1588. Finn Preston's story was foolproof. The only men who might have proved it false had died a long time ago.

Still, there were these other chests waiting out at The Fangs . . .

He sighed, and reached for the telephone.

# *Author's Postscript*

SANCTUARY ISLE, its characters and incidents, belongs to fiction – though I know and respect the men who run its real-life counterparts.

But the Armada is fact – as is the unloading of treasure from the galleon *San Salvador* to a smaller ship in mid-Channel, the wrecking of Armada ships near or around the island of Mull, and the trickle of survivors from points on the Scottish and Irish coasts who finally returned to Spain. The Tobermory galleon is not, say some experts, the treasure ship of legend. Bids to salvage it have been described as being of 'archaeological purpose.'

The location of two other galleons is believed known, and along the Argyll seacoast there has long been the story of a fourth vessel, one which went down at a spot which . . . but let's leave it at that.

For now, anyway.